City of Belief

For Raona —

With enduring friendship —

then and now.

Love,

Nicole

City of Belief

a novel

Nicole d'Entremont

Fox Print Books

ISBN: 1. Catholic 2. New York City 3. blackout 4. protest 5.
sixties

Creative Commons
559 Nathan Abbott Way
Stanford, California 94305, USA.
Published by: Fox Print Books
45 Pleasant Ave
Peaks Island, ME 04108
foxprintbooks@gmail.com

To Alexander Putnam Cole and the future

Author's Note

In the early morning hours of November 9, 1965 a
young man walked up to the United Nations in New
York City, sat on the cement island on First Avenue before the darkened building, doused himself with gasoline and lit a match. The young man was Roger La
Porte and he was my friend. Only hours before, he and
I and another friend were eating hot dogs in Weitzman's Deli down by the Williamsburg Bridge. A light
rain was falling, almost a mist, and I was annoyed and
disturbed that Roger was with us. Three hours earlier
at Roger's request he and I had had a private conversation. We stood on Kenmare Street in front of the
tenement apartments the Catholic Worker rented for
its volunteers and then at my insistence because the
same light mist was falling, we went into the tiny foyer
between the exterior doors and the door leading to the
first floor landing. It was too small a space to contain
what was being said and I remember pressing my back
into the wall. That conversation, Roger's later immo-
lation, the events of the evening of November 9, 1965
have haunted me for over 40 years.

In crafting this novel, I have kept faith with the
chronology of events as I have remembered them. Some
of the dialogue is taken whole cloth from remembered
conversations. In some instances, I have conflated sep-
arate people into one character. Most names have
been changed. Significantly, Roger La Porte appears as

Jonathan Le Blanc. I did this initially to shield Roger's remaining family from re-entering the pain of these events but later realized another motivation. Changing his name and others freed me to enter more fully into the emotional world of the people presented. The historical figures of A. J. Muste and Dorothy Day, however, are named.

The habitués of the Bowery I have named generally by the monikers bestowed upon them by that bygone era: Italian Mike, Mad Paul Bruno, Smokey Joe, Frances Furpeice, Whiskers, Louie the Hat. This book is also for them.

March 2009

Preface

It was a story lost on the night everyone remembered. The war in Vietnam had settled like a relative who came for supper and stayed forever. It had its own room by now and had sent out for extra clothes. It promised to go every day, find a job, get an apartment. But, it stayed, making the guest room its own, eating the family food, falling asleep in front of the television, snoring through the late evening news, sightless to the images burning on the streets of Saigon and deaf to the daily tally of dead and wounded. It was a slovenly spectacle and everyone wanted something done about it. Jonathan was one of those.

— 1 —

Beginnings

The West Trenton Local began its plunge under the
Hudson River. Adèle Evangeline Dion, Del, as she preferred to be called, pondered her reflection in the window beside her. She liked what she saw. She looked
young and beautiful and anguished, her eyes dark and
brooding, her lips full. She was wearing her London
Fog trench coat with the collar up. She thought of
Humphrey Bogart and Ingrid Bergman and felt doomed
and heroic. The train's onrush through the pitch-black
tunnel lent a deeper darkness to what she knew to
be the outside night. She had been away from the
Lower East Side for the weekend staying at her family's home in the Philadelphia suburbs. When she was
a child the area had been rural but then the 50's happened and that world was erased by shopping malls
and gasoline stations and suburban developments. Her
house had become a solitary outpost of non-conformity
with its glass walls and brick living room floor and tree

1

trunks holding up oak support beams. Her parents left Philadelphia during the middle of the Great Depression and homesteaded this once burnt out farmland. Then in the 50's her father started to make money and, being an admirer of Frank Lloyd Wright, he built this home for them. Del loved the house but not the suburbs. They seemed an infection and the lives within their grasp, contaminated.

Life was black and white for Del and had grown more so after she moved to New York City, to the Lower East Side, to the Bowery. She felt the train starting to slow its momentum, breaking, coasting, stalling and then stopping completely. Soon. Soon. Del's real life would begin again. Her sepia reflection in the window had vanished, replaced now by someone more ordinary looking with long brown hair pulled back and held with a clip, a pimple on her chin that she was doctoring. Her blue eyes, she knew, were bloodshot.

"You've got very patriotic eyes," Doctor Gottleib had said. "Ha. Ha. Red, White and Blue." She had seen him this weekend for her six-month check-up. He handed her some new wetting solution for the contact lenses he had prescribed. The contact lenses were bourgeois, Del knew, but she loved them and saw much better with them than the framed spectacles she had worn all through college. The contacts were a gift from her parents and were supposed to be a graduation present but Del hadn't graduated. She left. She left college and she left the Church. Her parents were philosophical about college but her mother, a convert to Catholicism, was upset about the Church. Del counted herself lucky in this regard. Others of her friends had been kicked out of the house for less. Both her parents were concerned about where Del was living but she visited home once a month taking respite from her "philanthropic work" as the local paper had once seriously described it. She didn't like troubling her parents, though, and was glad she had three younger brothers at home for them to worry about. It took the edge off.

People were filling up the train's aisles now and dragging their luggage off the overhead racks. It was Sunday evening and weekenders were returning to the city: students, some families, businessmen getting a jump on the Monday rush. A little over an hour ago Del had kissed her father goodbye at the railway terminal as he stood alongside the idling station wagon. Hugging her, he had pressed a ten-dollar bill into her hand saying, "Take a cab." Dell fastened the top button of her London Fog, grabbed her bag and merged with the other bodies into the underbelly of Penn Station. The smell was of cinder ash and steam and smoke. The human throng. She ran upstairs and grabbed the A train. Getting off at West 4th Street, she walked east the rest of the way, through Washington Square Park to Little Italy, to home, to her new life.

Arrivals

Del first met Jonathan in the soup kitchen as she spread newspapers down on the long kitchen table. He was sitting between Whiskers and Mary Dillpickle and across from Italian Mike who made googly eyes and said, "Hey you! You wanna bust in the mouth?" Then Mike, grabbing his tit, struck a beefcake pose. Del scowled but loved it. Catching Jonathan's eye, she knew, he was hooked.

A few weeks later she heard he quit school and was staying with a friend down by the East River. Jonathan had wanted to move right away into one of the apartments The Catholic Worker rented but they were all filled, and, anyway, he hadn't proven himself. He'd have to clean toilets, get nits in his shiny hair, slime through crates of spinach before he'd earn that right. The organization had entrance requirements; anyone wanting to stay would have to pass muster. But, Jonathan was affable. He could wait. He didn't seem to be in a rush, at least not then.

Del didn't see that much of Jonathan for the first few weeks. Besides, he had taken to hanging out with Mercedes, a new volunteer who was living in the women's apartment next to Del's. Del didn't particularly care for Mercedes so when she saw them hanging out together laughing after dinner, getting cozy, then walking out the front door, she thought, let them, what did she care.

For Jonathan this ability to meet and enjoy women should have settled suspicions about his having been in a monastery. Anyway, for men in prisons, armies, monasteries, wasn't it normal to have sexual doubts? And, here was Mercedes, this girl with honey-blonde hair leaning her head into his shoulder and he feeling that fleeting pressure and then glancing sideways at her profile and seeing how her hair fell. They walked over to Ratner's on Second Avenue for tea and a cherry-cheese and then the conversation turned to Africa.

She had been known in her former life as Sister Mary Blaise but now in "the world" she was again Mercedes McCann, though answering to that name made her year in Africa seem even more a dream. Jonathan looked up from stirring his tea.

"That's all the time you were there? One year?"

Mercedes leaned her head against the padded booth and smiled.

"In Africa, that's all that's needed," she said. "There wasn't time there anyway. Not the way we know it. It could have been a month or a hundred years. I don't think I slept much in Africa."

She laughed a high-pitched, skittery sound. She was playing with the cherry-cheese they were sharing. Then, pointing her fork, said, "Your turn."

Jonathan told his story, abbreviating huge chunks, then said that after discovering Saint Jude's, he could never go back to the Monastery.

"Too removed." He drew his hand through his hair and tugged at the sleeve of his sweater.

"Here is the Church," he said. "Here. In the Bowery. The Body of Christ? Here. His blood? Here. I feel it every time I hand out clothes to the men. I'm real here."

For a moment he felt foolish. This outburst. His face was flushed. But Mercedes was nodding. She had felt the same in Africa, the disconnect between her vows, her religious life and the lives of the women and girls she taught in the village.

"Mother Superior thought I was going native," she said playing with what remained of the pastry. "Well, yes," she laughed. "Why not? After awhile, I just didn't see the point. The women wove such beautiful cloth. Why not wear it? What's the harm? But, that was the last straw. Not that I had stopped going to Mass because, *How could your God be more in a building than in the sunset?* That was just one of the questions the women put to me that I could not answer. "But," and here Mercedes shook her head, "it was not wearing my habit that finally did it. Mother Eubaldus was furious. 'To give up your religious garb, your sanctified cloth?' I did like my convent name though. I thought about keeping it, but decided to return to Mercedes. What do you think?"

"It's better than Eubaldus, that's for sure." Jonathan was finishing the last few crumbs and smiling. "My God," he said. "Where do they get those names?"

But, he knew. Had he stayed in the monastery, Brother Felician would have been his chosen name. He had originally wanted Finian, after reading James Joyce, but another monk had that name. Felician sounded similar, but by that time, Jonathan knew he wasn't going to stay.

Sitting in Ratner's now, across from Mercedes, it all seemed so right. He should be here. She should be here. There was all this work to do and, now, a place to do it.

Jonathan pulled out some crumpled dollars and paid the bill. Tomorrow, he'd help make soup, but, now, he would extend his arm and see a girl safely home before picking up a pack of cigarettes and walking back to the East River apartment.

— 3 —

Smokey Joe

Smokey Joe had been sitting at the front desk of the Worker for 15 years and had seen volunteers come and go, but, unlike Italian Mike who saw everyone as either a "goomba" or a "fruit", Smokey gave latitude. Perhaps it was his previous years in the merchant marine or maybe the war. What the hell did that Ginny do in the war, anyway, that's what Smokey wanted to know. Here the Ginny sat on his fat ass all day, scaring visiting nuns by pretending to have a heart attack, grabbing his chest and then diving for his prick. Naw, Smokey thought, the Ginny was a "shirker," pure and simple. Years ago he usta go get bread in that busted up baby carriage of his. Now, maybe, he'd lay some spit on a stamp for the newspaper mailing but that was about it. As for the new kid, Jonathan, maybe he was a fruit. He was good looking enough to be one. Maybe he liked the girls and the boys. Smokey'd seen that, too, and what a bloke did on his own time for his own pleasure as long as he paid his way was his business and his alone.

Smokey was dragging on his third, after-dinner cigar-ette and staring out the big, front window, the one Tim had just patched up from Arty's thrown brick. Maybe spring triggered it, first-of-the-month checks, a full moon. Any of those things. Smokey had his slips, too, but not on his watch, and he was down tonight to help close up the House. He knew he was a drunk and that cigarettes and coffee got him through the day and that was fine by him. Maybe, once a year, he'd let himself go on a toot but not bad like the Russian there who'd live in his own puke-soaked clothes day after day and whose hair stood up like he'd grabbed a live wire. Naw, when Smokey drank, he stayed in the apartment. Once in awhile he'd roar into Saint Jude's and then Tim would take him home and make sure he stayed. One time back when Smokey had his own place, Tim even laid over a few days when Smokey had the shakes. You don't forget that. Ever since then Tim was his matey even though the kid was a draft dodger like the rest of them. Not that this war was anything like Smokey's. Still, it was your country. Smoke feathered up and over his head and out the screen door mixing with fumes from a passing truck and with whatever sweetness was beginning to bud in Sarah Delano Roosevelt Park and beyond on Forsythe Street. Tim walked by and tossed a pack of Bugler onto the desk and Smokey pounced on it, scooping it up and pulling back his fist to fake-punch the air.

"Thanks, Timmy. You don't forget. Not like that Rufus there from California. Gave me fuckin' Prince Albert the other day." Tim looked over his shoulder and laughed. "Rufus, oh yeah, plays an autoharp. I suppose you set him straight."

"Yeah, yeah," Smokey growled. "Set him straight and the Ginny giving him googly eyes. Says the kid's another fruit for the basket and then starts actin' like one hisself."

Tim jiggled his eyebrows Groucho Marx style and twirled the unlit cigar he was holding close to his lips. "Waste of breath. Only people worth slandering are the ruling class." He winked at Smokey who growled again.

"None of that commie stuff, Timmy. We need a MacArthur, that's what. Not these panty-waists we got in there now." Tim dug deep into his pant pocket and pulled out a wooden match, striking it on the heel of his boot. Lighting his cigar, he tilted back his head and blew out a plume of purple to join Smokey's puffs.

"I'm with you on a lot of that, Smokey. Let's get outta here. I'm beat and want to catch the game on the tube with my gal."

"She like basketball, Timmy?"

"She doesn't know diddly about the game." Tim took a few more puffs and smiled. "But, she likes me."

"Yeah, I seen that. She's Ok. Still wears a skirt. Not like that beatnik, Blossom, there. I'd be worried, you was with her."

Tim pulled the dangling chord on the last overhead light and cuffed Smokey on the shoulder. "No need to worry, Smokey. Blossom's not my kinda babe. At least, not now. Let's go."

The two walked in silence down Chrystie Street to the corner of Delancy and, then, turning right, stopped at the Bowery. Ragged men were working the lights, getting yelled at for smearing dirty cloths on windshields. A garbage can fire burned on the opposite corner. Huddled forms around that fire passed a bottle. The traffic light changed to green and Tim and Smokey walked passed it all. Tim was whistling softly and Smokey felt himself a lucky man to be who he was right now walking home after a day's work.

— 4 —

Where They Came From

Most of the younger volunteers who came to Saint Jude's during the mid-1960's were in their twenties and from the middle class, a few were working class, and almost all were white. Tim was from Four Corners, New Jersey, Ray from Newark, New Jersey, Mercedes from San Francisco, Suzanne from Westchester County, Del from outside Philadelphia. Dewey was from Louisiana and Jonathan from Tinker Lake in upstate New York.

They were the sons and daughters of the World War II generation determined to settle down into the normalcy of post-war prosperity. Their fathers carried briefcases or lunch pails and came home to dinners prepared by wives who shared a drink in the living room or made sure cold beer was in the fridge. It appeared a safe predictable world, but many of these young chafed at its false solidity, listened to Elvis, snuck down to bars or beatnik hangouts in the city and many, if they went to college, eventually dropped out. Some joined the civil rights movement in the deep south and, later, as the war in Vietnam continued, became part of the growing anti-war movement seeking out places of organized resistance like The Catholic Worker and Saint Jude's. In the case of Saint Jude's, if you stayed long enough, cleaned enough toilets, listened to Italian Mike, Scotty or the Famine, didn't blanch when Frances Furpiece unraveled her stained leg bandages at the dinner table, then, that someone could, maybe, get a bed in one of the several apartments the Worker rented for its volunteers in Little Italy.

Del lived in such an apartment. The building was on the corner of Kenmare and Mott several blocks off the Bowery and the first night she slept there, she awoke the next morning with welts on her legs and back. Jumping out of bed, she tore off the sheets, ripped off the pillowcase. On the wall behind the pillow, she discovered, penciled in a spidery hand on the cracked plaster, a single Rilke quote, *"Who among the Heavenly Host would hear me if I cried aloud?"* She dressed and walked over to the soup kitchen, the Rilke quote refusing to leave her alone.

After the soup line was done at the House, Tim helped her wash her bedroom floor and walls and spray the bed frame and mattress. They took the sheets and blanket to the Laundromat. After, they walked down to the Lucky Grand in Chinatown and ate egg foo yung and fried rice and, much, much later, ended up at the White Horse in the Village for a couple of ales. That night she slept soundly and the next morning awoke to realize she had acquired for the first time in her life, a real boyfriend.

— 5 —

Who They Lived With

Sadie and Crazy Mary also lived in Del's apartment, plus there was always an empty bed available for a guest. That space was currently occupied by Marlene, a self-proclaimed nymphomaniac, who came and went but soon would be asked to leave since she kept bringing men home in the afternoons. She said she couldn't help herself, the dogs drove her she said, but, according to Miss Bean, the matronly British volunteer who supervised the women's apartments, "We're meant to be a shelter for the wayward not a brothel in which to be wayward. Poor thing, she'll have to do that elsewhere." But, Marlene had been gone for a week now and neither Miss Bean nor Del had seen her at the House or exiting any of the bars on the Bowery. She could be anywhere: Bellevue Psychiatric, The Women's House of Detention, or, though no one wanted to say it, the city morgue. "No news is good news," as Miss Bean said. "We'll pray for her soul."

15

Miss Bean was an anomaly to Del. She had been an Anglican nun before converting to Catholicism and seemed so proper and Brit, totally out of place on the Lower East Side. But, the men on the line loved her. Maybe because of World War II, maybe she reminded them of some Sister who dampened their brows in a London infirmary. Who knew? The men listened when she gave her brisk commands, as Del had once witnessed. "Put down that knife, Johnny, like a good boy, and I'll make you some tea." And, don't you know, but Johnny did and crying to boot put his head on Miss Bean's lap as she rubbed his back with, "There, there," while instructing Del with an exaggerated mime of mouth over Johnny's cradled head to, "Call Bellevue." Thirty minutes later Johnny meekly walked out with the attendants when they arrived and Miss Bean and Del finished the pot of tea and then Miss Bean instructed Del to go outside and get some fresh air because she looked white as a ghost. It had been a wonder to behold, Miss Bean's competence, and from that day on Del was always grateful when fussy, old Miss Bean was puttering around Saint Jude's, especially if Del were alone in the kitchen and preparing an evening meal.

Del felt the incident with knife-wielding Johnny, who turned out to be mad as a hatter, illustrated how much she thought she knew but how ignorant she really was. She had been around the soup kitchen long enough to know that most drunken fights usually ended with the wind milling combatants flat on their asses, but the cases of mental illness were another matter and they unnerved her. Service to the poor, when Del pondered it in college, had a nobility that in reality was not always present. She knew now that poverty smelled bad and that it was noisy and crowded, and in its extremity, was driven mad with alcohol, drugs and pain. It may look ennobling when one contemplates, *the lilies of the field* and *the least of these*, but it was often crazy and lost. She felt it could drag her into that. It was people like Miss Bean and Sadie and Smokey and later Louie the Hat who would keep her, on more than one occasion, from getting lost herself.

— 6 —

Discovery

New York City for Del was an incredible geode she had cracked and now was walking within. There was Madame Le Rou and her twenty-year-old son Jean-Claude. Both were crazy, no doubt, but Madame had an eerie aliveness. The storefront they lived in on Spring Street, along with their dog, Bonne Chance, was a hovel yet Madame was planning a mural on the south wall where the oblique north light, she said, would be, "entrancing". She had, she claimed, once played first violin for the Argentine National Symphony though the Count, alas, had left her with only a silver engraved cigarette case and, that, pilfered by some scabrous miscreant.

Jean Claude at the mention of "cigarette" would implore in a sibilant whisper, "Maman, a cig-a-rette?" He crouched in a corner at the rear of the storefront, his long arms encircling his legs, miming a smoke, two fingers pressed against his lips. "Maman, a cig-a-rette?

Please? Please, Maman?" To which Madame would hiss, "Hush, you bastard child." And then she'd return to talking about the mural or the Count while Jean Claude whimpered in the background. The exchange was repulsive and hypnotic. Del brought over two woolen blankets one afternoon to their place and never went back, but they would come regularly to the House for evening meals.

Then there was Scotty, harmless and eccentric, who on lazy afternoons at the House would wave his thumb in the air and talk about "me saber wound" on that very thumb, the result of his service in the Crimean War. She believed him. His wild white hair and rolling burr were all the proof she needed.

Sadie, on the other hand, knew Del as one of the young "bleedin 'arts" around the Worker and would scoff in disbelief at the stories Del would listen to and apparently believe. But, Sadie gave Del earfuls, too, that Del tucked away. There was Sadie's marriage to her wild-catter husband who worked the oil rigs in Oklahoma and South America, his early death leaving her impoverished, no social security, losing her home, coming back to the old neighborhood in the Lower East Side, but, "It's changed, changed. It used to be nice. Drunks and hoors, now," and she'd look off disgustedly, shielding her eyes from the glare of the overhead bulb.

Del imagined that for Jonathan, who had grown up in the country, Saint Jude's must have also seemed a fantastic discovery. But, his discoveries seemed more spiritual than hers. There was something about his religious inclinations and the life of the city that fit together perfectly. If faith in God and in the Church was a belief in things unseen, then New York City with its horrific discordance, beauty nesting in squalor, was the place to test that faith. Wasn't the shattered bottle on the Bowery caught in the afternoon light not beautiful? Wasn't that bread in the Bowery man's hands trembling over the coffee cup not a Consecration?

Jonathan remembered Father Alphonse, the pastor at Holy Spirit in Tinker Lake, taking him aside after the afternoon Benediction saying, "Look. Look at Our Lord in the tabernacle. Where is He? Not in the gold of the monstrance but, there, there in the simple bread. That gray wafer behind the shimmer of glass. That's where God resides."

Jonathan saw the man's eyes shine and his mouth tremble. Something moved in him then, and later that evening at supper when his family was still together, before his mother and father had separated, he brought up for the first and last time how he was thinking of becoming a priest. The look in his mother's eyes and his father's, "Pass the potatoes" and his brother's derisive hoot had ended any discussion. But, Jonathan knew. He knew, on that particular afternoon in the sanctuary, that he had turned a corner and that his life was now on a path away from the laboring life of his father, away from the scholarship his mother prayed for and away from the army his brother would eventually join.

His path was different and it had led him here to Saint Jude's. But, "here" was a funny place and he felt that he would be tested and would need to measure up.

7

Measuring Up

It was an early summer morning when Del knocked at the adjoining apartment to get the grocery list from Miss Bean. Dorothy Day opened the door. As the legendary founder of The Catholic Worker Movement, Miss Day was often away on speaking trips, so Del looked surprised when motioned inside by the legend herself. Del usually steered clear of Dorothy Day when she was in town. There were always too many people hanging around for Del's tastes and Miss Day had a way of staring that reminded Del of a rattler. Not that Del had ever seen a rattler, but there was something in Dorothy Day's heavy-lidded and direct gaze that unsettled her. Del stood in the kitchen fidgeting with a pen in her hand and said she needed to pick up the grocery list from Miss Bean. Dorothy, her cane in one hand and daily missal in the other, responded by asking if Del would first like to accompany Miss Bean and her to morning Mass at Old Saint Patrick's on

Mulberry Street. When Del mumbled, "No thank you," Dorothy immediately asked her if she went to Mass and received Communion. After Del admitted that she did not, Miss Day gave her that look, shook her head and said, "You'll never be able to continue this work if you don't." The awkwardness was mercifully broken by Miss Bean who bustled in, handing Del the grocery list having added powdered milk and one of those, "nice little tins of mandarin oranges if you have money to spare." Del took the list and the accompanying money envelope. With her hand already on the doorknob and avoiding Miss Day's eyes, she said, "I'll go right now. See you back at the House." She walked straight down the stairs and out onto Kenmare Street.

Sanctimonious old biddy is what Del thought. What did she know? Del did the work. Had done it for almost a year now. Cooked the meals. Worked in the clothing room. She was no Dorothy Day and did not want to be. What did she know about Del anyway?

Since it was early morning, the heat hadn't hit the sidewalks. Usually, Del enjoyed walking down Delancey to the Essex Street Market at that hour. She liked the light feel of her new Orchard Street sneakers and the breezes that fluttered up and under her blouse. She was no nun, not by a long shot. She didn't want to end up like them.

Anyway, going to the Essex Street Market was every bit as sacramental as kneeling in Church. Old meddler. When was the last time she gave out clothes in the

women's clothing room? Crossing the street Del saw
Jonathan walking up the other side of Delancey. He
would be going over to the House. Sometimes this city
was just too small. She didn't want to be working with
him today. He asked too many questions.

The wide door of the Essex Street Market opened
to an interior as cool and shadowed at this quiet hour
as the inside of a Church. Automatically, Del unfolded
her list in front of the butcher's stall. First item. Ten
pounds chicken feet. The butcher winked and left returning moments later. He pushed the bloody bag of
feet over the porcelain countertop.

"So, gimme the scratch?" A joker in a gore-smeared
bib. Del fingered out two bills and rooted for change as
he said. "Forget it. Get outta here." He was a nice guy
who more than once threw in extra hamburger or pork
chops. With the remaining money, she purchased the
other items and Miss Bean's mandarin oranges; then,
still brooding over Dorothy Day's words, she headed
back to the House hoping that since she was down to
cook, she wouldn't have to put up with both Jonathan
and Mercedes wanting to be helpful. These thoughts
continued pestering her until, pausing at a curb, she
noticed a thin rivulet of chicken blood dripping me-
thodically onto one of her new, white sneakers.

By the time she arrived at the House, the line was
over and Jonathan and Mercedes were sitting at the
front table sharing a sugar and margarine sandwich.
Whiskers immediately jumped up and rescued her from

the bleeding bag of chicken feet. Walter, downstairs for his mid-morning tea, remarked on her sneaker's ghoulish, Jackson Pollock appeal. Walter was an artist and had an eye for such things. He collected dead horseshoe crabs and painted them so they resembled primitive masks and hung them in the third floor office space. He said they reminded him of Rouault's stained glass windows. "And they smell like shit," Dennis said who was over by the sink doing dishes. "And, what do you know about art?" snarled Walter flouncing his way up the stairs, mug of tea in hand.

While walking back from Essex Street, Del had decided to extend herself to Jonathan and Mercedes and ask if they would help peel potatoes and onions for this evening's meal. Also, she wanted to find out if they would do dinner tomorrow. It would be Friday, a macaroni and cheese night, so they couldn't go too wrong with macaroni and cheese. Besides, it was time they did a meal solo.

Happily, the afternoon went smoothly and also the evening meal, the only dispute being one between Mad Paul, who collected the leftover table scraps to feed the birds, and Jonas Sassafras, who insisted on saving all the eggshells for Ed so he could clarify the coffee for next morning's line. The argument escalated with Jonas's shrill accusation that Paul cared more for, *the birds of the air* than we who are made in God's image and Paul's rejoinder that Jonas resembled a life form decidedly below what God's image implied.

Ed, who had the House that night, and who was always the voice of rationality in these disputes assured Jonas that he already had eggshells saved in the refrigerator and then Miss Bean interjected that pigeons received abundant calcium from pecking the sidewalk. This remark made Paul's upper lip curl, confirming, yet again, the supreme idiocy of women. Del decided not to stay for Compline, the evening prayer of the Church, the one religious practice at Saint Jude's that she loved. The day had already been too long and with Tim away at a War Resisters Conference, she was hoping for a quiet evening at home.

8

A Quiet Evening

The apartments the Catholic Worker rented were cold-water railroad flats, remnants of the area's turn-of-the century immigrant past. The tub was in the kitchen, and the water closet, outside on the landing, was shared with two other apartments. From what Del knew of the history of the Lower East Side, she didn't think much had changed in those apartments from when whole families from Eastern Europe lived within those walls. Only, now, in this particular apartment the current immigrant inhabitants were all women, each coming from worlds as different from one another as the New World was from the Old Country.

That evening upon opening the apartment door, Del was greeted with a returned Marlene, naked except for a sweater wrapped around her waist, standing upon a chair in the middle of the kitchen, screwing a light bulb into the overhead socket. Sadie sat on the couch puffing out disgusted huffs of air while tugging at the house-key pinned to her dress. Crazy Mary was over by the stove making tea while muttering French verse.

Concentrating, Marlene flicked her tongue in and out through a gap where her two front teeth had once been. She was happily humming as she threaded the bulb. Closing the door behind her, all thoughts Del had of a peaceful bath and a quick to-bed vanished. Marlene went, "Ah ha!" as the 60 watt bulb cast dusk into the room.

Sadie released another puff of air and poked her chin in Marlene's direction, "Crazy bitches and bums and hoors. She had one of *them* in here this afternoon. I heard it."

Mary, abandoning her French, said, "That was Charles and me, you old sack. We're married and enjoy conjugal rights. More than Miss-Goodie-Catholic-School-Girl over there with her little twit squeaking the bed springs."

Del knew Mary was convinced that she and Tim were doing it like rabbits. It was hopeless to protest that despite all Tim's efforts she was still virginal. Crazy Mary particularly disliked Del and had largesse only for Marlene and the dogs that drove her. Del's cheeks flamed as Marlene motioned her over and rested her hand lightly on Del's head steadying herself while stepping off the chair. The pressure of the hand, though light, sent a whirring sensation through Del's body and Marlene's exposed breasts frightened her. Marlene was

laughing, "Thank you. Thank you, Mary, but no need
to protect. Yes, I did have a fine tumble here this afternoon." Mary, pressing an open palm to her cheek,
turned her face to the wall and spoke with low fury.
"Carnality. Slime. Filth. Corruption."

Sadie, rolling her eyes, shifted her weight upon the
crackling newspapers she had put down to make the
couch prophylactically safe. Shielding her eyes from
the bulb's dim glare, she let out a long slow exhalation,
"So, you want some coffee, Della Del?"

The remainder of the evening was spent in relative
silence. Sadie and Del sat together on the couch. Mary
mumbled behind the curtain in her room. Marlene had
gone out having first freshened her armpits with tap
water from the kitchen sink and then slipping on the
nylon blouse she had rinsed out and dried on a line
strung over the gas stove. The room was quiet. Sadie
and Del sipped their coffee. Sometimes, sitting there
when the apartment was thus, Del liked to imagine
that other past when the rooms were filled with those
other immigrants. She imagined everyone home from
the docks or the factory, the water being boiled for
Saturday baths, the diapers hung over the stove and
the smell of pirogues and sauerkraut. There would be
crying and laughter but still it was far, far better to
be in this land of possibility and dreams than in the
Kaiser's army or, later, the camps. Much, much better
to be alive and working in the sweatshops, as hellish
as they were, because, still, you were able to go home

and be with·your family. These were thoughts Del had, especially when she wondered if she would ever have a husband and children and diapers and all that yeasty chaos instead of living with crazy women.

Sadie had started to snore with her head thrown back on the couch and her bottom lip quivering. She had taken down her hair releasing it from the tortoise shell combs that were a prize gift from her late husband who had made good money in his day working the oil fields. Del knew this because Sadie often told the story of the money earned, squandered, made again, lost, the little home in Oklahoma with the white, picket fence, the chickens because they couldn't have children. Then, one night, while reading the evening paper, his slumping over. "Just like that, dead," said Sadie. "Dead. A good man like my husband. Drunks and hoors that live. Can you figger that out, Della?"

Of course, Del couldn't. And, of course, there would be hell to pay if she even attempted an explanation. So, Sadie slept with her head tilted back, her hair feathered out over the top of the couch, beautiful hair, a mix of rose-gold blonde and white, her scalp pink as a baby's. Del was struck by Sadie's hair and with the turquoise shell combs resting beside her opened palm, the unconventional beauty of the world surprising her again and again.

— 9 —

Tangles

Friday night Del heard about the macaroni meal. First, Mercedes had picked through two crates of spinach but in the process threw away most of it, so, when boiled down, only about six cups remained to feed 40 people. Jonathan got the macaroni right but he forgot to go to Saul's to pick up bread for the morning line so no bread could be spared for the evening meal. Scotty threw a fit because how was he going to, "Make me sandwich?" a ritual performed every night regardless of the menu. Mercedes did manage to salvage the meal, however, by going out and buying ice cream, bananas and Hershey's chocolate syrup. Del thought it cheating even though the action did circumvent what could have resulted in a major revolt.

Del got the lowdown from Sadie who had eaten at the House and been escorted home by Jonathan. Sadie had taken a shine to him, calling him, "My Honey." She had pet names especially for the men around the House.

Del's boyfriend was, "Banty" and Edmund, "Crewcut."
Almost all the regulars at the House had a nickname. It
seemed to Del a carry-over from another time, a speak-
easy era. Sometimes she felt she was in a 1930's film
that kept spooling out and tangling about her feet in
the 1960's. Her own past was filled with stories her parents had told her of their coming of age in the thirties.
The men on the Bowery looked like the out-of-work
men her parents described in Philadelphia. The huddled forms Del saw in doorways on the Bowery were
the same forms she had been told about who slept outside by steam grates in the Philadelphia winters to keep
warm. Even her own coldwater flat was reminiscent of
the rooms her parents described that they had lived in
while students at the Academy. How many times had
she heard of living on peanuts and apples and five dollars a week. But her parents' stories lacked the smell
of poverty or the dirt or the anger. Maybe they didn't
want her to know or maybe they had suffered their own
young time with adventure and hopefulness. In any
event, Del often felt these woozy inter-splicings. Their
wars were different though. Her parents' war was beginning in Europe in 1935 while Del's in 1965 was firmly
entrenched. Her parents did not support the Vietnam
War, however, and that made Del different from most
of the young men and women she knew. When she
would talk to her new friends she heard more than one
story of mothers and fathers feeling disgraced by a child
seen in a demonstration, growing a beard, dropping out

of school. The mothers usually tried to placate the fathers, but, in the end, many children either got involved in draft resistance or dropped out or went to Canada or, sadly, sometimes tragically, enlisted to put an end to the argument. Everyone paid a price.

That spring and summer saw increased anti-war demonstrations in Washington, and in Vietnam there were heavy U.S. losses. More than once, Del thought of Yeats's poem, *The Second Coming*, and conjured *the rough beast* referred to making its way across the land, urgent to be born. The war seemed futile and inexorable. *The ceremony of innocence* was drowning. They were all caught in the flood.

For herself, if she became consumed with these or other melancholy thoughts and was lucky, someone at the House would pull her back from the brink with an angry shout or a request for more coffee or maybe there'd be Smokey's raspy, "Did Timmy give you the keys to the closet, Del? I'm outta Bugler." Then, the world snapped into focus and she would return. But, if Del were unlucky and no one wanted anything, she would have to live with that gloom which sometimes provoked ill-advised walks at foolish hours.

— 10 —

Love-Fest

Both Jonathan and Mercedes had a good laugh over the macaroni meal. Del, though, remained incredulous about the tossed spinach and made snide comments the next day about people throwing away perfectly good produce. Jonathan caught Italian Mike doing his googly eyes at Del and then simultaneously they all heard another voice singing out, "She's on the ra-aag!"

The voice belonged to Brother Sixtus who emerged from the pantry, hands extended like a surgeon's awaiting disinfection. Sixtus, pronounced "Sextus" by many at the House, had spent several years in monastic life and had a phobic fear of germs. Rumor had it, he was called "Sextus" for his inordinate affection for the monastery sheep, a character flaw that supposedly led to his expulsion and subsequent showing up at The Catholic Worker.

Several feet away from the pantry, slouched on a bench, was a gaunt, lank-haired figure who appeared to be in a stupor but who now lifted his head and shouted, "Shut your yap, sheep-fuck." Del was minding the kitchen for Miss Bean while she was away doing afternoon errands. The Saturday Shepherd's Pie was slowly cooking in the oven so Del knew Miss Bean would return, but the afternoon looked in danger of unraveling and Del knew Mercedes and Jonathan would be of little help. Tim was due back today from the Resistance Retreat but Del didn't expect him until late evening. Anyway, he and Del had had an argument right before he left and their relationship was on unsure ground. She was irritated with him and didn't want help from that quarter.

She shot a dirty look over to Brother Sixtus who was doing ablutions over an empty bowl and then aimed a similar stare at her defender who again appeared slouched in stupor. She sighed and, feeling a twinge of guilt, took advantage of the quiet to go over and apologize to Mercedes for her short temper about the spinach. Mercedes laughed, waving away the apology with, "Maybe that's why they never let me into the convent kitchen."

Jonathan leaned into Mercedes jostling her shoulder. Then, entering into this temporary love-fest as if on cue, Tim came back early from the Retreat and Del, sick of seeing Jonathan and Mercedes cooing over one another, forgot all resolve and shamelessly gave Tim a big hug and kiss right on the lips which got Italian Mike going and led to the abrupt departure of Brother Sixtus and the appearance of Smokey who said, "Missed ya, Matey," and, also, Sadie who came down the stairs because she heard, "My little Banty, heard his whistle."

Tim soaked it all up saying from now on he was going to go on retreat every month if this were the kind of reception he could expect upon return.

— 11 —

The Resistance

That evening Tim and Del closed up the House. After
paying Art and Scotty into the Sunshine Hotel, they
walked down to the Lucky Grand in Chinatown. It was
a beautiful evening for a stroll and being with Tim felt
so comfortable that Del thought maybe it could work
after all. They paused at several Mott Street storefront windows filled with rows of carefully layered fish
on ice chips. Glazed chickens hung in their mahogany
skins. Golden Buddhas grinned from open restaurant
doorways. Incense wafted. Red banners fluttered. Chinatown, in its everyday finery, wooing them again and
again.

The Lucky Grand was a dive from the outside. It
had rickety, wooden steps leading up to the restaurant's
second story entrance. The stairs swayed as you walked
up to the landing but once inside, the place was rock
solid. At this hour, it was crammed with Asian families
and municipal shift workers, cops in uniform and now,

the peaceniks, to round off the bill. Tim knew a few words in Cantonese and shouted them out to one of the waiters over by a large, round table near the swinging kitchen doors. Folks of all ages were sitting at the table digging into a huge platter of steamed shrimp. The waiter, patting his vest pocket, laughed and pointed toward the kitchen shouting something back to Tim who nodded and returned the "patting" gesture.

"What's that about?" Del asked. Tim assumed his "cat that swallowed the canary" expression and from his shirt's vest pocket pulled out a cigar. He twirled it under his nose and smiled, "Primo. Old Lum, the cook, loves these." Tim explained how Manny at Westside Smokes had just gotten in a new cigar shipment from Havana via Hong Kong. "Isn't it great?" he said, his hazel eyes twinkling. "The All-American, immigrant, entrepreneurial, subversive spirit. *Embargo? What's that?* Old Lum will go nuts over this."

Tim was fired up from the Retreat so Del knew she was going to hear her fill of left-wing exuberance. The waiter came over and Tim deftly transferred the cigar to him saying, "Complements to the Chef." They ordered their usual: egg foo yung, chicken fried rice, side of bok choi, crispy noodles, extra duck sauce and spicy mustard which Tim firmly believed was good for his gut. It all came with pots of tea and, later, extra chicken fried rice for Mr. Tim's table from Old Lum.

They stayed eating and talking for a long time, Tim filling Del in on events: the position papers, the arguments, the storming out of rooms, the caucuses, the unknown guy from the West Coast, who everyone thought was a plant, who tried to get a T-Group going and then demanded a vote on the issue. Augustus, the other Catholic Worker attending the Retreat, fuming, said he wasn't going to stand for that California crap. Fearing a distracting brawl, Eric, from the War Resisters League, talked Gus out of the room. By the time they both returned, a vote had been taken on that issue so Gus was furious all over again even though as an anarchist he wouldn't have voted anyway. Gus was new to the Worker and possessed an authoritative air. He was a few years older than the rest of the younger volunteers and also had been an English instructor before losing his appointment after picketing his local draft board. He particularly irritated Tim by referring more than once to possessing a perfect knowledge of English grammar.

Del felt this all went on and ridiculously on but she could see Tim was relishing the telling. He especially enjoyed the story of Albert from the 5th Avenue Peace Parade Committee splitting his one vote in half with Rico, who had just been thrown out of his Chapter of the IWW, so that each of them could cast a one-half vote in favor of the resolution permitting the North Vietnamese Liberation Front flag to be flown in the next demonstration.

Tim, almost out of breath, lapsed silent while taking a swallow of tea and scooping out another wedge of egg foo yong. Del wanted to know the outcome of the "flag" vote so Tim filled her in complete with snatches of heated debate. He leaned back in his chair and patting his stomach summed it all up with, "So, let every flag be flown: The Socialist Workers Party Flag, The Progressive Labor Party Flag. Even the goddamn Anarchist Rhino Flag."

"And how did you vote?"

Even as Del asked the question, she knew the answer. Tim leaned forward in his chair smiling; as usual, slow to pick up on the tone of her voice.

"You know me, Babe."

"No," said Del. "Refresh my memory."

"In the end, if one flag flies, they all should fly." Tim's eyes were twinkling again as he jiggled his signature Groucho Marx eyebrows.

"Or none should fly. Why didn't you say that, Tim? You just cave in all the time." Del felt her words thud onto the table. They were right back into their old argument, the very one she and Tim were having before he left. He had backed them up into it and, now, it was too late.

"There's a difference between caving and compromising, Del."

Tim put another dollop of mustard onto his plate. "I know where to draw the line."

Del frowned and sipped her tea. She thought Tim and Gus were worthless at the Retreat. Why did they even go? They were supposed to offer a fresh vision where no flag was slavishly followed ever again. Now both of them had dropped the ball: Gus out of anarchist anger and Tim, out of laissez-faire laziness. That's what Del felt.

The walk home was silent, Tim sensing that something had gotten badly away from him again. He asked Del if she wanted to get some suds at The White Horse or maybe go for a ride on the ferry, but she weaseled out of the invitation by saying maybe tomorrow. When they got back to Kenmare, she gave him a perfunctory goodnight kiss and once inside her apartment leaned against the closed door listening to him slowly mount the stairs to his room three flights up.

— 12 —

Not Tonight, Pal

She was so goddamn self-righteous. He should go out
and get laid. Bad enough he had just spent all week
with a bunch of horny, anti-war, fixin'-to-die dudes, all
of them working on their position papers and ready to
hurl their puny selves, *onto the gears of the odious ma-*
chine, a phrase that Rico loved to borrow from Berke-
ley's Mario De Savio. Tim pulled back the curtain to
his bedroom and stripped to his skivvies, new ones his
mom in Four Corners had sent to him.

Four Corners. He couldn't believe he actually came
from a place named Four Corners. He looked down
at the line of light brown hair on his belly trailing a
straight path to his root, his thing, his dick, the family
jewel encrusted rod. "Not tonight, Pal," he mumbled
to himself. Jesus, what a disappointment, not just her
downstairs or the gal at the Seventh Street Pub he knew
he could bed any night of the week, certainly not Larry
whose soulful eyes had followed him all during the Re-

treat and who patted his rump whenever he could, but all of them together and he not getting any. He peeled off his skivvies and shook himself out.

Do you wear your jock-a-lot? Good old Fugs. AC-/DC. At least, they were getting some but he didn't swing that way, he knew it. He pulled on a pair of baggy, green surgical scrubs he'd gotten in the men's clothing room and kicked his jeans into a corner.

His room, such as it was, had a double bed mattress on the floor. It took up most of the space, touching points on all three walls. Over and against the fourth wall hunkered a Philco 36 inch scratched up walnut television console. On top of that was a small, framed snapshot of his mother, father, himself and baby sister taken on a trip to Atlantic City fourteen years ago and a framed lithograph of Karl Marx. Tim sat on the edge of the bed and rolled a joint. He needed to think about his future. He'd like to get married. He hadn't asked Del yet but it had been on his mind. He drew a long pull of the sweet grass. She was such a Puritan. If she were here now and he passed her this joint, she'd take this little, sippy toke and then hand it back. Well, more for him but he wished he could loosen her up. She was better with booze. Last time he visited Four Corners, he brought back a bottle of Applejack and they almost killed the whole thing mixing the shots with cider. He'd gotten her bra off then and he knew she could feel the bulge of his cock against her thigh, but she stiffened when he started to inch his zipper down. Blue balls. Great Balls of Fire. Damn. He took another delicious pull. He had to satisfy himself with just her titties. Small but mighty. She said he was like a mewling, little kitten, but he knew she, at least, liked his mouth there as she swelled and groaned. He cackled to himself. "Stoned. Poor bastard."

He flopped back on the bed and felt himself, trying to get a response, but he was too zonked to rise to the occasion. He remembered a mother cat they had at home once when he was a kid, her swollen teats and how after awhile she ran from her litter, all those scraggly balls of fur tormenting her. He tried to get the image out of his mind, turn the page, but it stuck there tangled in the smoke and sheets.

Sadie's Sacrament

Del's apartment was quiet at two in the morning. She was saddened about the turn of events with Tim but things were going nowhere with him. She knew he was probably up there now rolling a joint or polishing off the apple brandy. She quickly pulled back the curtain to her room and clicked on the small light on the night-stand. Her room consisted of a bed, nightstand and an armoire at the foot of the bed all positioned along-side the passageway that connected Sadie's room with the kitchen. It was the smallest room in the apart-ment, but the other alternative was to share a larger room with Crazy Mary and she was not about to do that again. What could have been the biggest draw-back was that the passageway alongside her bed was the only way for Sadie to get to her room. But, they had worked out their accommodations, and, strangely, they mostly worked. In the morning, which now would be in about four hours, Sadie would lumber through clutching her jars of evaporated milk and Chase and Sanborn Instant Coffee, shifting her weight from one leg to the other and grumbling under her breath about, "the nuths 'n hoors" and about how someone who was pretending to be asleep should go back to *her people.*

Sadie would place both jars on the tub lid, and God help anyone who hadn't replaced it if a bath had been taken the night before. She would then open the refrigerator and get out a saucer of margarine and a loaf of Wonder Bread. She would grunt her way over to the stove and turn on the oven full-blast, then pull off the kettle and fill it with water all the while grumbling about, "Crazy, crazy bitches and hoors."

Mary would also be awake at this hour and listening behind her curtain. She would know to stay put. Sadie would measure out her instant coffee and wait for the water to boil. Del would hear the scrape of the spoon on the side of the cup. She would stand in front of the stove since with her bad legs it was hard to be popping up and down like a jack-in-the-box for the goddamn coffee that, at least, she had gotten away from the bums. When the kettle whistled, she'd say, "Jesus, Mary and Joseph. Jesus, Jesus," until she'd have the kettle off the stove and the boiled water poured into her cup.

It was like this every morning. Del would hear Sadie rummaging for the sugar bag in the overhead kitchen cabinet, hear her mutter, "Run, run, bugs, bugs, cock-a-roaches, little bastards" as she'd scare the vermin back into their cracks. She'd put a spoonful of sugar into her cup and crumple the bag closed. Then, she'd lumber back over to the couch alongside the stove, open the oven's door to let out its hot breath and sitting down with a grunt would first savor the silence and then after a sip of the hot liquid say, "Jesus, Jesus. Good," followed by a sweet smacking of lips.

Lying in bed now and worrying about Tim was getting Del nowhere so it was a comfort to think of Sadie and her morning routine. If Sadie were in a good mood, she might make toast for the two of them. She had done so before, placing four slices of Wonder Bread on the broiler pan and turning them golden, then placing several pats of margarine in the middle so the toasts would be puddled to perfection. If Sadie were in a good mood, this might happen today. Something was needed to start the day. Maybe it would be Sadie's sacrament.

— 14 —

Mercedes

Mercedes still couldn't figure out why Del had gotten
so undone over spinach. She felt it was a minor glitch
in an otherwise amazingly smooth day and everyone
had been delighted with the ice cream sundaes. She
did admit that in her prior life, she had been accused
by Mother Superior of being extravagant but felt this
was different. She was not in Africa and this was her
own money. Anyway, wasn't she supporting the local
economy by going down the street to the bodega and
buying ice cream and syrup and bananas? Del had
agreed to this last part though grudgingly. Mercedes
suspected Del still saw it as grandstanding. She remembered Del listening in on a conversation she was having
with Jonathan when she admitted to him that in Africa
her Mother Superior had accused her of having a willful
and extravagant nature. She overheard Del mumbling
under her breath, "She got that right". But what did
Del know about Africa? Nothing. Africa was Mercedes'

world.

She had been stationed in Musoma in Tanzania. Her job was to teach religion and English to the girls and women of the village. She had been shocked by the poverty but, at the same time, humbled by how generous the villagers were with the few possessions they did have. This was the society she was to redeem for Christ? No wonder she felt on more than one occasion unworthy to kiss the hem of Musoma's garment.

When she spoke of these thoughts to Mother Superior, she was admonished about the temptation of false pride. Then, when she experienced her first bout of despondency, Mother Superior cautioned her about the dangers of, "morose delectation", the willful delight in melancholy thoughts. As her term of service continued, Mercedes found herself cycling between two extremes: a sense of boundless, exuberant energy which would energize her so she wanted to do everything both for and with the women and girls and then, when those feelings and activities were spent, listlessness and bouts of weeping and lethargy. She found herself in those times hard pressed to participate in the life of the religious community or the village. After one such trying spell, she was sent to a retreat house on Lake Tanganyika in hopes that a change of scenery might settle her. But she developed a malignant fever there that would not relinquish its hold and eventually after mystifying both the doctors with her physical ailments and her spiritual advisors with her cycles of elation and malaise, she was sent back to the States, to the Motherhouse, 30 pounds lighter and, as her mother said, "looking a fright." After visiting her daughter in Chicago, her mother insisted on a return home to San Francisco, so Mercedes took a leave of absence from the Order, packing her bags one evening and unceremoniously letting herself out by a side door entrance.

Within six months, she had gained back almost all of her lost weight though she was still visited by occasional fever and chills. Also, during that time and after sufficient reflection, she officially left the Order she had pledged her life to, packed her bags once again and, against her mother's wishes, left for New York City and Saint Jude's.

— 15 —

Jonathan

Del supposed Jonathan was drawn to Mercedes because
he had some of the same preoccupations, some of the
same questions about what God wanted him to do. But,
unlike Mercedes, he had more urgency.

Del remembered the story he told her about Father
Alphonse, his parish priest, and what happened after
Benediction. Jonathan said now he was at Saint Jude's
he understood what the old priest meant. Now, he
knew in his own flesh that the gray, nondescript wafer
of bread within the Monstrance was the Christ whose
body had been rent, bones numbered, blood shed so
that, he, Jonathan Le Blanc, might live. Indeed, he
had once, after Sunday Mass, thought he felt the Par-
aclete enter his body in a rush of wings. He went on
describing the sensations, the fluttering filling his ears,
a faintness overtaking him so much so that Del couldn't
stop herself from asking if he had forgotten to eat break-
fast that morning, but Jonathan let the sarcasm slide

and said simply that what he felt then in the Church
of the Holy Spirit was real and akin to the poetry of
Gerard Manley Hopkins.

It was the imagery of skylarks and windhovers come
alive and careening in spiritual free-fall. Yet, it was also
a vision rooted in the fleshy flawed natural world. It
was right here. He said he knew this and Mercedes
knew this. And he thought Del did too. And, now,
at Saint Jude's, they could live it. Christ in the bread
broken in the Bowery man's hands and in the ecstatic
rush of wings was more visible, more attainable than
ever.

— 16 —

The House

There were two societies existing at Saint Jude's and when they were good, they were very, very good and when they were bad, they were horrid. When they were good, the House ran smoothly. The men on the line did not get into fights but moved slowly and dug their hands deeply into their greatcoats looking like photos Del had seen of the breadlines during the Great Depression. On good days, the House would feel like a church with muffled conversations and shuffling feet and when the men sat down there would be the scrape of cutlery in bowls and the low vibration of eating and breathing and little conversation. On days like this, the volunteers would speak softly, too, and maybe there would be no conversation at all except to say thanks and pass this or that and maybe a gentle kidding of Edmund for always putting eggshells in the coffee grinds, a trick he learned during the Korean War. The conversations would sound intimate and people would treat each other more like couples who after having a terrible fight were making up and being tender with one another. Those were the good days.

The bad days saw broken windows, cartwheel punches and someone gently but firmly shown the door. On bad days, everyone seemed to yell and nobody seemed to listen. Maybe it was full moon or the SSI checks were in or one of the volunteers handed out Bugler instead of tailor-mades to the wrong person or it was a lousy meal or Mad Paul wasn't getting good scraps for the birds. Any of these events could turn things sour and voices would be raised and objects thrown. Those were the bad days.

Regardless of the tenor of the day, whether good or bad, the society that came first and foremost at Saint Jude's was the House family. This family was different from the men on the line or the occasional man or woman paid into a flophouse. The family lived in apartments rented by Saint Jude's. It consisted of the volunteers, the "bleedin' 'arts" as Sadie put it and the men and women of the House who had been there longer than any of the volunteers and who had seen volunteers come and go. These were people like Sadie and Smokey Joe, Missouri Marie and Mad Paul, Italian Mike, Frances Furpiece, Scotty and Mary Dillpickle. These were people with names and lives to match the names. These were also people like Miss Day, who was a legend, and Edmund who had fought a war, and Miss Bean who was old enough to look a man in the eye and shame him into handing over a knife. These were people who had lived. As for the young volunteers, they were good kids and they were "our kids" even if the young men were draft-dodgers who should cut their hair and get a job, and the girls should go back to suburbia, marry a doctor, get knocked up and wheel baby carriages around shopping malls. Still, good days or bad, they were *our* kids.

Of course, Del didn't know this then, though she suspected it, suspected that they were the children. Even though the children were the ones paying people into flops, handing out clothes and making dinners, they should still mind their elders or have their ears cuffed verbally for being smart-asses. They, of course, would only listen half-heartedly to such admonitions. They had important work to do.

Kids

And who were these children and what was the important work they had to do? They were Ray, Dewey, Jonathan, Tim, Del, Mercedes and Suzanne, all of them in their early twenties. Augustus and Edmund were the old men, 27 and 48 respectively. And, there were others. Some would come to visit from college and stay a few days or weeks; some would drop out of school completely and wander; some would eventually go to Canada. Some young men who visited or volunteered would become consciousness objectors but most would go to jail for refusing to have anything to do with military conscription.

And the work? Keeping the House going, cooking the meals, going to the market, handing out clothes, taking folks to Bellevue, writing for and hawking **The Agitator**, Saint Jude's monthly paper. And, all the other "goings" here and there in an attempt to end the war: going to demonstrations, going to schools to talk about the draft, going to jail.

For Del's own part, she had not officially dropped out of college though that is what she called it. More accurately, she had not returned after completing her senior year having failed repeatedly to pass a required math course. For her, there had been no traumatic scene with her parents about wasting their college investment, no angry words or casting her out of the house as with Ray. Her parents voiced their concerns about where Saint Jude's was located but not about the work. They were also against the war and maybe even happy that she was at least remaining close to home and hadn't joined the Peace Corps as did another of her college friends.

That was not the story with most of the young people at Saint Jude's. Most had stories similar to Ray's whose parents were flat out angry and bewildered. Also with Ray it was intensified due to the fact that his father had recently garnered a big Defense contract and was now, instead of manufacturing containers for optical equipment, constructing packaging for fragmentation bombs so they would arrive safely at their destination. Ray, noting the irony, would practically spit out the words when he gave talks about draft resistance at local colleges and universities. He told about how his dad threw him out of the house and took down his high school graduation photograph and tossed it into the fireplace replacing it with his older brother, Bill's, official Marine-In-Dress-Uniform photo, placing it on the mantle along with his Honorable Discharge. "That's what my old man did." Ray would conclude talks like that and then abruptly sit down.

Now, Ray and Suzanne were playing a waiting game for his Induction Order to arrive since he had recently been re-classified 1-A. He was hoping it and his subsequent arrest would not happen before he had a chance to burn his draft card publicly in Union Square this fall along with Gus and Tim and members of the War Resisters League.

— 18 —

Protocols

In those days, the events leading up to an arrest and conviction for draft resistance generally followed a certain protocol. Initially came the act of refusal either privately of an induction order or publicly at a demonstration. Either action would insure an indictment being handed down by the courts, then the arrest order, the arrest itself and whether or not to resist that arrest, the arraignment, bail set and whether or not to accept that bail or to assume a "jail-no-bail" position. If one were offered and accepted release on bond or personal recognizance then a decision had to be made about whether or not to obey the requirement forbidding participation in further demonstrations. If one broke that order, the consequent arrest would mean additional charges. Then, of course, there was the whole matter of whether to accept legal counsel or argue your case yourself. So it was: the indictment, the arrest, the trial, the verdict, the sentencing and, finally, serving jail time of usually three to five years' duration. It was a predictable and sickening progression and Del never saw a judge look anything but irritated or bored. She hated seeing the backs of her friends being led out of a courtroom. Three or five years later, they returned, muscled-up and bitter.

Their own pre-courtroom protocols consisted of parties and endless conversations about how to handle the authorities. They would generally gather in the men's apartment late in the evening with potato chips and ale. There would be a record player with Dylan rasping out *A Hard Rain's A' Gonna Fall* or Ray would savage his twelve-string with *Ain't Gonna Study War No More.* The rest of them would listen or join in on the chorus. Sometimes at the end of a song when all of them had joined in, a great silence would settle upon the room and they would look at one another and not know what to say. In another life, they could have been college kids celebrating the end of exams. Instead, they were celebrating someone about to go to jail just as somewhere else in the city another group of friends were tossing back beers for one of their own shipping out to Vietnam.

Once, during an impromptu party when it looked as if Ray might be imminently arrested since the FBI had been asking questions in his hometown, Suzanne got up and left the room while he was reading what he intended to say in court. He was talking about freedom and the wind in his face and the love of friends and she got up and left and Del followed her out the door and down the hall and then down the four flights of stairs and out onto the street and it was there Del learned Suzanne was pregnant and what about the lilies of the field now?

"No, Ray doesn't know," she said. She had just gotten the results that afternoon from the clinic. And, yes, she'd keep the baby and she thought Ray, once he knew, would want the same and, then, the conversation stopped. She'd tell him later on tonight, she said. Del thought Suzanne shouldn't be eating at Saint Jude's anymore and she'd, of course, have to stop smoking and what would they do about jail? This Del blurted out, "How can Ray go through with that considering this new development?" But, Suzanne said, "No. That won't change. He'll go to jail. He'd hate me and the baby for the rest of our lives if he couldn't go to jail."

Birds Of The Air

In college if you wanted to lay a chick, you hung a necktie on your doorknob. At Saint Jude's, you went up to the rooftop. On a sweet spring night in April, Ray and Suzanne had mounted the stairs to the third floor of Saint Jude's and then climbed another series of very narrow steps leading to a raised bulkhead and unlatched the door to the rooftop. Suzanne was the first to see a star and she felt Ray's heat behind her. She stepped out onto the warm tar and took only a few steps away from the entrance, keeping well away from the edge of the roof yet still feeling vertiginous. Ray hitched himself up and pushed the door softly shut behind him, securing the lock as he was told to do since this was the first time he had ever been up there.

They both stood side by side getting their sea legs and looking out to Delancey at the traffic moving toward the Williamsburg Bridge and then turned to look across Chrystie into Sarah Delano Roosevelt Park resting peacefully in the city's gathering dark with the trees bending in a feathery breeze. Ray held an old sleeping bag, a green canvas backed one with flannel inside of deer racing in the snow. He spread it out on the rooftop alongside the flank of the bulkhead. He sat down and took off his jacket and laid it down next to him, patting the spot and looking up at Suzanne.

She noticed he was wearing a new t-shirt that appeared moth pale in the street light. She thought he was like a youth in a Botticelli painting she had once seen in art class. He extended his arm and she took his hand and saw the strong blue vein leading up to his heart. She looked at that and then into his eyes, deep set and dark and then the gloss of his hair as he bowed his head while she knelt on the sleeping bag and she put her fingers into his hair and felt its spring and tilted his head back and kissed him on the mouth struck by its softness and also by the fact that she did that and then he looked at her with a question in his eyes and placed a finger at her breastbone and traced a line down her cleavage and undid a button and kissed her there and she felt the sky tilt more than the earth move and for both of them it was a first time and she knew whatever happened between them after this, nothing could take that away.

— 20 —

Nabbed

As it turned out, it was Dewey the authorities arrested the next day. The party had broken up around one in the morning and Del remembered setting her alarm clock for five-thirty. She had promised Tim she'd go over early with him to the House along with Ray and Dewey. Edmund was taking a break from Sunday morning duty and that meant coffee needed to be made and the soup prepared. Plus, Ray and Dewey were going to get the House car and drive down to the Fulton Fish Market to see what they could score for the next week's meals.

Even before the alarm rang, Del heard Sadie poking around the kitchen. "Jesus, Jesus, cock-a-roaches. Filthy, fuckin', little bastards." She was up early also, getting ready to go out to the Island, to the lady there who gave her house cleaning work. Sadie went every month even though her legs were bad.

"You want coffee, Della Ella?" Sadie was in a good

mood, what with the prospects of a few dollars and a nice lunch. Del said no, that she needed to hurry and get dressed since Tim would be at the door any minute.

"Oh, my little Banty, cock-a-roacha. I didn't hear the bedsprings last night." Del knew Sadie imagined all kinds of acrobatics going on and were Del in a less pre-occupied mood she would indulge the banter, but this morning she just mumbled, "No spring action last night, Sadie."

"Jesus, Jesus, if I was with that little Banty-Jesus, Mary and Joseph, that's not what you'd hear."

Del had gotten up by now and pulled on the same skirt, turtleneck and sweater she had been wearing a few hours earlier. The kettle was boiling and she heard Sadie making her coffee just as she heard Tim whistling and coming down the stairs.

"Oh, Oh," said Sadie. "Here comes my honey, cock-a-roacha." Tim knocked and Sadie let him in. Snatching her toothbrush from the nightstand, Del parted the curtain to her room in time to see Tim in his Irish fisherman's sweater fending off Sadie's fake grab at his crotch. She was commenting on how his pants hung low on his hips and he was loving it.

For a little guy, on the scurvy side, Tim exuded a flirtatious, gun-slinging energy, part of his wild colonial boy persona, with an early morning, reddish stubble on his chin and dirty blond hair falling into his eyes. Toothbrush at the ready, Del entered the kitchen and giving Tim a quick squeeze around the waist moved between him and Sadie on her way to the sink. Tim winked and Sadie made note of how momentarily their hips had brushed in passing and started up again with, "Oh, Baby, Baby now we're talkin'. That's the way to start the day."

Tim agreed and then they all heard Dewey and Ray outside the door and with a quick knock, it swung open and Ray leaned in with Sadie calling out, "Oh, more cock-a-roaches. Where's that Jumbalaya boy with the white teeth and crocodile smile?"

Del heard Dewey's muffled reply from behind Ray's back, "Mercy, save me. I'm justa' sweet, innocent, country boy."

Del brushed her teeth, splashed water on her face and moments later with Sadie mid-sentence, grabbed her jacket and Tim's arm and said, "We're off" and with a push and a wave, all clambered down the stairs and out onto the street.

It was the last week of August and fall was already in the air with its chill and sharp delineation of light. They all went "Brrrr" and Tim said he was glad he put on his sweater and Dewey said he wished he had one and Ray said, "Let's check the clothing room when we get to the House and see what we can find." Ray was shivering, also, in a short-sleeved shirt, the hairs on his folded arms standing up straight and his shoulders hunched as if to keep whatever heat was in his body from flying up the street. The sun was hitting the buildings on Delancey turning their outlines copper bright. The four of them walked two abreast towards the Bowery, quiet now and enjoying the quiet, the smell of roasting coffee drifting in from somewhere, an older Italian man sweeping the sidewalk of the scungilli joint, a cat bounding down an alleyway. At the Bowery, they looked both ways. No cars except for one cabby racing uptown, the traffic lights at this hour stalled on green as far as you could see. They got midway to the cement island and then sprinted across as the light changed. The rest was a blur.

Two black sedans squealed around the corner to a stop, doors flung wide, three men jumped out all wearing, Del couldn't believe it, identical hats and trench coats. What's going on? Dewey thrown against the side of the second car. Badges flashed in front of their faces. FBI. Ray lunging at the agent who was pinning Dewey to the car. Thrown back. Tim and Del frozen. Dewey saying, "Take it easy, man." His arm twisted behind his back. "Even if I had the damn card, I wouldn't be able to pull it out to show you." His crooked smile. Jambalaya boy. Crocodile. Shoving Dewey into the back seat of the second car. Ray throwing himself on its hood.

"I'll have to arrest you, too, Son, if you do that." A beefy hand on Ray's shoulder. Tim talking to Ray, pulling him off. Doors slamming. Dewey's face peering out the rear window, grinning, flashing the peace sign. Then, an arm flung, the back of his head, two bodies on either side. The cars roaring up the Bowery. Gone.

The three of them standing there. Then running, running to the House.

— 21 —

Miss Day

Dorothy worried about the new crop of young people
arriving at Saint Jude's. The recent Dewey Dubois
incident with the FBI's high jacking him and his subsequent jailing on charges of draft refusal was her latest
upset. The authorities had flown him the next day to
New Orleans escorted by Federal marshals. Upon ar-
rival he was driven to the Acadia Parish lock-up and
thrown into the drunk tank where he immediately had
part of an ear torn off since he was a, "goddamned,
nigger-lovin' commie." Ray asked Dorothy for bus fare
to New Orleans and went down for the sentencing. It
was quick, no jury, and a five-year bit to Parcher Penitentiary. Before he left, Ray visited Dewey in Parcher
and said Dewey was more shaken than he had ever
seen him but glad it was over, glad, even, that he was
in Parcher since most of the inmates were black so at
least he didn't have to worry about being carved up
by some good ol' boy. Ray returned paler and quieter

than usual.

But as disturbing as Dewey Dubois's arrest was there was something more that troubled her. The Catholic Worker had always attracted the young and searching but this current wave was so young and the search for most of them had so little to do with any spiritual inclination. Some were even corrosively hostile to the Church and carried within them a barely concealed contempt that she found unsettling. Before her own conversion to Catholicism, she was angry, yes, but it was at the State. For religion, she had, at best, an indifferent shrug. She felt its threats were soporific compared to the State's wickedly energetic ability to wage not one but already two World Wars within her lifetime and continually align itself with a capitalist system that squeezed the life blood out of men, women and children. In her own youth, she had fought mightily against the State, written thousands of words in left-wing periodicals, been jailed more times than she could count. But, these children mostly had known comfort and safety. They had not lived through a Great Depression but been sheltered in the suburbs, and even those coming from the working classes had laboring fathers and mothers who provided enough to eat. Even if they were genuinely poor, their destitution was not that of previous years, Roosevelt had seen to that and though she had her ideological arguments with his reformist views, still, he had seen the need and provided this limited solution. The safety nets were in place for these war babies though she knew it was fraying, could see the signs.

And, now, this new war as sinister and ambiguous as the Korean conflict preceding it was demanding its pound of flesh from the young. But these young, more cynical and suspicious than their parents, had started disobeying way before some politician began talking about falling dominos. The young ones weren't buying it, but she worried that they did not have the resources to stay the course. They arrived with copies of Sartre or Camus tucked into their back pockets. If they professed any religion at all, it was Jesus as Revolutionary, but they had so little faith and the Sacraments, though there for them, were scoffed at or ignored.

Just as the other day when Dorothy asked Del if she would like to go to Mass and Del declined, the look the girl gave her, nervous and defiant all at once. And then when asked if she ever went to Mass or received the Eucharist and Del said, "No," Dorothy felt what she had felt so many times with these young people, a sinking wash of feeling, you will not last. Something sad and prescient ran through her and she could not restrain herself from saying, "You'll never be able to continue this work if you don't."

She didn't mean to chide, but she knew how the girl took it responding only with a shrug and then with Miss Bean's list in hand, she was out the door. Dorothy prayed for her at Mass. To Del's age at Dorothy's age, she did not know what to say except her own truth.

— 22 —

The Wedding

Dewey's arrest and swift sentencing was a slap of cold water for them all. Ray and Suzanne had been especially affected and after Ray's return and with Miss Day's blessing and financial help, they rented their own apartment on Prince Street and two weeks later were married. The wedding was held in a small church on Broome Street where a particularly gruesome Jesus hung crucified over the altar. Notwithstanding, the service was lively with Ray playing the guitar, finding folk songs that had a wedding feel to them, *This Little Light of Mine* and *Rockin' In My Sweet Baby's Arms* which passed, though a digression, as far as recessional hymns were concerned. Both Ray and Suzanne's parents attended looking alternately bewildered and accepting. They, at least, remembered when to sit, stand and kneel during the Mass so it was fortunate they were seated in the front pew. Both sets of parents declined the offer to attend the reception held in the soup kitchen but later in the afternoon stopped over to see the newlyweds' apartment. Ray's father brought over a good bottle of scotch and Del saw them shake hands in a manly sort of way. Ray's brother, Bill, arrived late giving both Ray and Suzanne big bear hugs and a case of Ballentine ale. Ray's mother as yet unaware of Suzanne's pregnancy took Ray into the nuptial bedroom and presented him with a red, silk smoking jacket so he wouldn't, "Scare the girl."

Later, after the official family had gone, Gus cracked open bottles of Ballentine ale. Ray got out his guitar. Tim rolled a joint. Jonathan and Mercedes came over with left over cake from the House. They all toasted Suzanne and Ray. They toasted Dewey. They laughed about the parents. Ray modeled his new smoking jacket. Suzanne said she couldn't wait to be scared. More people came. Some people left. Del thought it seemed there was no war.

The War Front

On August 2, 1965, a Vietcong force made a full-scale assault at Ducco. U.S. First Infantry and 173rd Airborne Brigade were flown in and the Vietcong withdrew. TV news showed U.S. solders setting light to village huts with Zippo lighters.

*

On August 11, 1965 race riots began in the Watts area of Los Angeles. With the landing of advance units of the 7th Marines in Chulai, the U.S. Marines now had four regiments and four air groups in Vietnam.

*

On August 17, 1965 U.S. Marines destroyed a Vietcong stronghold near Vantuong.

*

In August 1965 President Lyndon Johnson signed into law a bill making it a Federal crime to destroy or mutilate a draft card. The new law carried penalties of up to five years in prison and a $1,000 fine.

— 24 —

Protest

Ray and Tim and Gus had all decided to publicly burn
their draft cards in Union Square. For Ray it was,
"This will force the issue." For Suzanne, it was, "Why?"
The draft board was already going to get him for re-
fusing Induction, why have two charges leveled instead
of one? For Tim, it was, "The law's unconstitutional.
Let's see what the old fool does in court." For Del it
was fear for Ray and queasiness for Tim. She could see
Ray being trotted off to jail and Tim cutting a deal.
Both scenarios were sad and demoralizing.

The draft card burning was being planned for an as
yet unspecified day in November, part of a nation wide
protest set to conclude with what organizers hoped
would be the largest *Stop The War Now March and
Rally* ever to be held in New York City. Demonstrations were also being planned for 40 other cities in the
United States as well as London, Brussels, Copenhagen,
Rome and Stockholm.

During the planning stage, the draft card burning
segment had been the focus of more than one, long,
heated debate with some coalition members feeling civil
disobedience should not be part of the official march
since it might scare some people off who would otherwise join the demonstration. Others felt that the draft
card burning should be the centerpiece of the protest
since it was the strongest statement that could be made
and was guaranteed to have maximum press coverage.
Del stayed for one into-the-wee-hours meeting until she
felt she couldn't bear to hear another mention of this
or that position or whose flag would fly where or which
group should lead the march or who should or should
not be invited to speak and what constituencies should
be represented on the flyer and who was or was not eli-
tist. She did note that very few women spoke except for
Bella Abzug and then all the men had the good sense
to shut up. A shaky consensus was finally reached after the tempering words of A.J. Muste who suggested
that the draft card burning be held in Union Square
on the day before the big march and that the official
march and rally down Fifth Avenue be held in the afternoon of the next day. That way energies would not be
dispersed since the whole weekend would become one,
long, sustained, "No".

Meanwhile life went on at Saint Jude's although
it would be false to say that outside events were not
taking a toll. Even Smokey, sitting at the front desk,
leaning on his elbows and sucking in smoke, narrowed

his eyes when anyone wearing a suit came through the door. Since Dewey's arrest there was a general skittishness about the House. It was also common knowledge that informants had infiltrated the peace movement. It would be simple to chalk this up as paranoia, but the fact was these people submitted signed affidavits for courtroom trials and often were the ones in demonstrations to incite marchers to break ranks or throw a rock. Del had witnessed this herself during a demonstration. A scurvy guy in an army jacket with a peace symbol inked on its back tried to get a group to break off and follow him into Sack's Fifth Avenue of all places with the charge, "Let's trash the capitalist whore-machine." Del had surprised herself by grabbing a retreating student's arm and saying, "Don't. The guy's a plant."

The agent–provocateur looked back, laughing and skipping on up the line, got lost ducking into a crowd of spectators behind the barricades. Creep is what Del thought. But, more and more, anti-war demonstrations were spinning out of control and silent vigils or visits to colleges where people actually got to talk instead of yelling slogans at one another were becoming things of the past.

— 25 —

Questions

Jonathan was also thinking about burning his draft card. He still had his student deferment but it was making him feel cowardly. At the same time, he was also entertaining the thought of enlisting, of becoming a medic, a non-combatant. Tim scoffed. "For what? Patch them up just to send them back. Why?" Still, Jonathan thought, a life saved is a life saved. What's done after is up to the person. Then he thought about his brother who had been in the army for two years and hated it. Jonathan knew he'd be upset by any mention of draft-card burning. He'd have choice words for that kind of stunt. He'd more help Jonathan go to Canada if he wanted out of the draft. Ray on the other hand thought Jonathan should just sit tight and not do anything since he still had his deferment. Anyway, someone had to hang tough with the House.

It was late at night as he thought these thoughts. He was stretched out on the floor of the room he now shared in the men's apartment and was leaning against his bed frame with James Baldwin's book, *Another Country,* open on his lap. Tim and Del were watching a Celtics game in Tim's room. He'd hear Tim whoop every so often and yell something to Bill Russell. Jonathan wouldn't even have known Del was in there except he saw her once pull the curtain back and leave, probably to go to the bathroom down the hall. She hadn't seen Jonathan because his bedroom curtain was drawn shut although he could see her through a thin break in the seam. He thought the Monastery more private than this place; at least, there, they had real doors. When Del came back, Jonathan saw her stand in the kitchen for a moment and look out the window onto Kenmare Street. Then, she patted her skirt and went back into Tim's room. She didn't seem happy. He and Mercedes had talked about this, more on the subject of Del being cool to Mercedes. He'd noticed it too but thought it was just Del's way. She had been so with him, he remembered. She practically bit his head off in May when he asked her if she'd been on vacation. He was in the middle of finals then and didn't know that she and Suzanne had been arrested and in The Women's House of Detention for a week. He'd been embarrassed when he found out from Tim where she'd been and wanted to apologize, but felt foolish so let it drop until things got better between them.

Then, a few weeks later, they were both stuck scrounging a meal together for the House and since someone had forgotten to order the meat, they had to go semi-vegetarian. They put together a pretty damn good stew with cream of wheat and tapioca thrown in as thickener and by emptying four bottles of Heinz tomato ketchup and a bottle of A1 Steak Sauce into half a dozen cans of tomatoes, a crate each of cut up carrots, potatoes, onions and, the secret ingredient, the contents of an industrial sized box of Bacon Bits. Everyone loved that stew and kept coming back for more. When they finished cleaning up the kitchen that evening, they went down to Jose's Diner at the corner and toasted their combined genius with a cup of coffee. Nothing was said but something had shifted and Jonathan remembered walking back to the East River apartment he still shared then feeling a lightness to his step as if he had just passed a test and finally received a good grade.

Tonight, though, he didn't know what Del needed, but, he knew, whatever it was, she wasn't getting it from Tim. He had his own thoughts about her as he had about Mercedes. He liked the company of women. In general, he preferred their company to that of men. He supposed this should quiet any sexual doubts he still might have, but he knew what people always suspected about men and monasteries.

When his thoughts went around and around like this, he generally went for a walk regardless of the hour. Maybe he'd just walk around the block or stand in a doorway he particularly liked on the corner of the Bowery and Kenmare and smoke a cigarette. It was there he prepared to take himself after Del parted Tim's curtain and went back into his room with Tim yelling, "Go! Go!" Jonathan could hear him slapping his legs. He picked himself up from the floor and put the book on the window ledge. He pulled on his sweater, tugged the overhead light and stood for a moment in the darkened room hoping that Russell would do something extraordinary so the roar of the crowd would cover his leaving. But, it was suddenly muted in there now and sounded as if the news were on or something, a modulation of voice, the daily toll of dead. He parted his own curtain and with quick soft steps was out the front door and onto the landing. He locked the door behind him making sure he pocketed the key. He patted his breast pocket for cigarettes and, satisfied, went down the stairs.

A light rain was falling as he stepped out onto the street almost like the mist that sometimes rose and hovered over the lake in Tinker. He pulled down the sleeves of his sweater. Then, by habit, he pushed them up again to his elbows. He pinched a cigarette out of the pack, put it to his lips, then took it out again, rolling it between his fingers as he walked toward the Bowery.

He was having a hard time shaking Baldwin's book with its central character caught in his own confusions. The mood clung to him like the mist, like seeing Del's look out the window, like Mercedes' words this afternoon when the knife she was holding slipped from her hand and she laughed, "Butterfingers. But, where's the butter?" He had laughed too and pushed the saucer of margarine in her direction watching her hand tremble slightly as she held the knife again ready to dig into the soft mound. She caught his eye and said, "I know. I know. I'll see a doctor." He didn't believe her.

Their relationship had settled into a teasing friendship though they still flirted outrageously, both of them trying on a role so denied in their prior lives. He was thinking now about friendship and the Baldwin book as he stepped up and under the overhang of his Bowery shelter. He leaned against one of two ornate pillars. He wondered about the building's elegant former history. The Bowery was a blasted landscape now. He put the cigarette back to his lips, twirling it on his tongue, trying out a rakish mood. Then, he struck a match and inhaled deeply listening to the sizzle of the paper, feeling the flutter of his heart. He felt he was in another country like Baldwin's character, not that he could ever deeply comprehend how a Negro could feel in a white man's world.

But, Jonathan did feel alien in his own skin sometimes and his country was becoming more and more alien to him the longer he stayed here on the Lower East Side. Tinker Lake seemed a lifetime away, too: his mother's scrubbed kitchen, his dad sitting in the Laz-E-Boy in front of the television, dinner at six-thirty, bed by ten, the tags on the dog's collar jingling, jingling as she scratched a flea before flopping down on the living room floor near the heat register. Home.

He looked out over the filmy street, a cab every so often high-tailing it up the Bowery trailing snakes of red light. Down the block three men fed a garbage can fire with busted up wood pallets. A bottle was being passed and, at this hour, no brown wrapper. Quiet. Very quiet. Peaceful even. Like church. Maybe the way church should be, he thought. Bread and wine, wherever two or three are gathered in My Name. Maybe he should join those men. Maybe he should bring the bread. The Monastery aspired to this but he was here and here is where it made sense, *Living* as Cardinal Suhard had said, *in such a way that one's life would not make sense if God did not exist.* Thoughts such as these energized him so that it was hard, sometimes, just to stay in his body, just to live. He needed to peel vegetables or hand out clothing. He needed that to nail down these thoughts so they wouldn't take off the top of his head.

Then there was the war and the draft. He took another deep, deep drag and let the smoke dribble out of his mouth and his arm fall to his side, the cigarette's glowing tip getting smaller and smaller until it singed his fingers and he let it drop, grinding out the butt with the sole of his shoe. He walked around after that, down to Chinatown just to calm himself and popped into the Lucky Grand and ate two egg rolls and slowly drank a pot of tea. It was four in the morning when he returned to the apartment. He went to bed with his clothes on knowing he'd be up in two hours to work the line.

— 26 —

Morning Thoughts

Dorothy Day liked her coffee black. This was just as well since the watery, blue, powdered milk at Saint Jude's did nothing for her. It repulsed her even, though she knew it was the milk of the poor just as evaporated milk was the cream. She considered this admission revealed a snobbish forbearance passing as virtue and wondered if she were getting sanctimonious in her old age. Maybe that was why the girl had looked at her that way. It was obvious that time when Del couldn't wait to get away and bounded down the stairs. Dorothy knew these young people worked hard at Saint Jude's, but they felt no need of prayer or the sacraments and she knew one could not sustain the hardships of this work without that support. She had seen the girl slipping into the church in the afternoons. She stayed only a short time and then would leave not knowing she had been observed. Dorothy often came to Old Saint Patrick's in the late afternoon sitting in the cool of the side altar's shadow. It was the time of day she most loved to pray and reflect. The girl did not know this or she never would have entered at that particular time, of this Dorothy was certain.

Perhaps she had been too harsh. Was she forgetting who she had been at that age? How many times before her conversion had she chastised religion, thought prayer a stuporous opiate of the people, its heavy pollen of forgetfulness settling upon the faithful, while, outside hunger marchers were beaten and strikers jailed? Worse yet, and this the girl would be sure to remark, not only did it appear that prayer dulled the senses but the Church openly disapproved of acts of civil dissent. And, yes, thought Dorothy, this was so and this her torment even now as conflicted as Christ's on the cross, *Why hast Thou forsaken me?* At those times it was only faith and only prayer that saved her, convinced her she was not alone and that God was working in mysterious ways, ways she could not comprehend.

But, she had not always felt this way. She had felt as these young people, needing only comradeship, the struggle, Joe Hill, the Wobblies, Debs and that is what she had done. Then, she had met Graham and been so taken with him, his way of speaking, his long walks in all kinds of weather, how he would stoop down, mid-stride, tenderly picking a flower, turning it over pointing to its stamen, following the vein and how she could not help in those moments but feel his finger on her own pulse and how that made every part of her tremble and how he looked so ravishingly like a photograph of Rupert Brooke she had once seen in her Anthology of British Poets. How Graham had laughed at that and dropped the flower and put his arm around her shoulders and every ungainly part of her seemed to fit with him and feel lovely. Then came the child and then the arguments.

She had been studying Catholicism on the sly. She wanted Cara baptized. They had a terrible argument one evening about God and Science and Religion and how could she be even tempted to believe that superstitious rubbish? Cara was baptized and then Dorothy herself and with that, the last straw, Graham left and so began her long, long life away from him.

Dorothy was used to her thoughts traversing in this manner and also used to the tears that sometimes made silent paths down her cheeks. She shook her head and dabbed her face with a handkerchief near the book she had been reading. The coffee was cold by now and she sipped its blackness as deep and brackish and fulfilling as the memories. Soon Miss Bean would knock on her door to ask if she were ready. Dorothy was going up to the farm this weekend for the annual Pacem In Terris Retreat. Hopefully at this meeting she would be able to sway the attending clergy to speak out more forcefully against the war. The hour was late and already she, too, felt the tremors, the beginning cracks in the anti-war movement. She had seen this happen too, too many times. The divisions, the name calling, the suspi-

cions, the accusations, the recantings, the whole movement collapsing and then, out of the rubble, McCarthy,
the witch hunts within and without, jail, suicide, friend-
ships lost and everyone's hand deep in the stain. She
knew the draft card burnings were going to happen and
she approved of them. She knew the FBI would be at
the door. She knew it would mean jail for the very
young people who were now serving dinner that night
to the poor. She knew it all and she approved of it all
and she counseled all to resist. But, she wished these
children could get down on their knees and pray so they
could last.

27

Tremors

Mercedes was in Bellevue Hospital. The initial visit was to stitch up a deep gash made while chopping vegetables for the evening meal. The knife had slipped, cutting her left hand's forefinger and thumb. The cut required sixteen stitches. The reason she was admitted, however, was that she didn't even know she had cut herself until Jonathan had rushed to her with a towel to staunch the blood. It was discovered then that she had known yet not told anyone that she had been gradually losing sensation in her hands and feet. Jonathan was furious, first at the hospital for having to wait two hours for a resident to stitch the wound, and then at Mercedes for having withheld that she was having, besides tremors, diminished sensation in both hands and feet. The hospital ran blood work after learning Mercedes had recently spent time in Africa and had had bouts of malaria. She was then checked in for observation.

Mercedes, herself, appeared unconcerned. She felt,

especially since Tanzania, that in these matters of health, things ran their course and resolved themselves. The fevers would come, would rattle your body with alternating gusts of cold and hot and, then, like a great torrent spending itself, would go, leaving you shaken but curiously calm and grateful for life. Illness had been that way for her even as a child. She remembered measles and the hallucinatory jump of shadow in the darkened room, the curtains drawn so only scant light would enter. How it seemed she was there for days and days, too weak to raise her head except to sip water through a straw. She remembered a cool cloth on her forehead, how it became almost instantly warm and then the cloth being changed and her mother's shadowy figure coming and going and the old doctor arriving and the cold stethoscope to her chest and the nauseating mix of cigar smell and rubbing alcohol as he leaned close to her and the scratch of his coarse wool sleeve on her skin. But, one morning, early, before dawn, the fever broke and she awoke, her sheets drenched and chill and, she, weak and cool and eerily calm. The malarial fevers had been like that also and, in a strange way, she took comfort in them, feeling they would come and then leave and the calm would return for a brief window and, maybe, something would be revealed to her, but this she did not say to anyone – the fact that she wanted, was looking for, expected even, some revelation.

Jonathan stayed with Mercedes for the afternoon

she was admitted and would not leave until he had seen her finish her evening meal. She felt vaguely irritated over his concern. This was hers she thought irrationally, hers, and she would take care of it herself. She joked with him though about eating all her Jell-O, the only un-overcooked item on her tray and about his provocative posture sitting on the end of her bed. She poked his thigh with her toe and said he should run along before anyone suspected further intimacies. The familiar flirtation completed, he leaned over and kissed her lightly on her forehead and eased himself off the bed. He was taking off for a quick weekend visit to Tinker Lake early in the morning but would come see her as soon as he was back in the city. He waved. She waved and then he was out the door. Mercedes closed her eyes and leaned back into her pillow allowing for the first time that she was supremely tired.

28

Going Home

No one was in the apartment when Jonathan returned. He was happy for this and entertained the idea of drawing a bath. But, the thought of Tim or someone else walking into the apartment while he was butt naked in a lukewarm tub of gray water was enough to have him forgo that idea. He supposed he'd need to get over this prudery eventually, but just the thought of sitting in a tub in a kitchen and having who knows who walk in was humiliating. He thought again that you definitely had more privacy in the Monastery and certainly more allowances for basic modesty.

Even as a kid, he hated any calling of attention to his body, so much so that when his brother would give him a wedgy, he'd have to find a private place to tug his underpants free. This made his brother howl even more while making farting noises with his hand under his armpit. It seemed he and Ted had been at each other like that forever until the time Ted nearly killed himself at sixteen by falling through the ice. Jonathan, tall at thirteen, had the presence of mind to flop spread-eagled onto the ice and grab his brother's curly hair in both hands and inch him toward the shoreline, breaking the ice forward until he had Ted's torso heaved onto the near bank. Then, he had slapped and raced him all the way home on the old logging road, having thrown away the almost empty pint of rum found in the sodden pocket of Ted's pea coat. By the time their folks came home from a Christmas shopping trip to Rochester, Jonathan had Ted pretty well sobered up and in bed, the wet clothing in the dryer except for the pea coat that he hid in the garage until he took it later to one of the big dryers at the Tinker Wash and Dry. The next morning his brother woke up with a terrible cold and a new found respect for a little brother who had some stuff beyond sissy crying at Lassie shows on television. Jonathan worried about Ted though not the way their mother did that Ted would do something foolish and get himself killed, but that he might keep getting into scrapes that needed someone to bail him out and Jonathan wouldn't always be there. He'd see Ted run through friends like that who became tired of digging into their pockets to pay for this or that fine or of receiving late night calls because Ted's car was in a ditch. Jonathan hoped this wouldn't be a lifelong thing. His father was always saying, "You can lead a horse to water but you can't make him drink." He'd say that and rap the kitchen table with his knuckles or slap the evening paper on the side of his leg. Sometimes he'd say it about Ted, sometimes about him, sometimes about his mother. It was an all-purpose proverb and finished more than one conversation before his father settled himself down before the television and the evening news.

Jonathan felt his father lived in a world as nuts and bolts as the ones he sold in the hardware store. If someone came in looking for roofing nails and the store only had wood framing nails in stock, Mr. Le Blanc would try and discourage the purchase. But, if the customer insisted, his father would bag the nails and later come home shaking his head saying, "Wait for a blow and that roof'll take off like a flying guillotine. Lead a horse to water but you can't make him drink." He'd rap his knuckles or slap the newspaper and then go fall asleep in front of the television while Jonathan saw tin roofs flying through the air slicing off heads like so many cucumbers.

Hearing Tim's whistle and footsteps on the stairs, Jonathan stopped wondering about drawing a bath. The apartment door swung open and Tim walked in carrying two quarts of ale and a bag of chips. "You like basketball, man?"

So, they watched the Celtics get creamed by the Knicks and polished off the chips and ale and Jonathan had his first tokes of Acapulco Gold. He woke up next morning at eight o'clock in Tim's bed, noting, with relief, that Tim was fast asleep in his. Later, he caught the noon bus for Tinker feeling surprisingly clear-headed and ready to take on the world.

29

Moving Swiftly

When Jonathan returned from Tinker Lake late Sunday evening, he learned that Mercedes had been formally admitted into Bellevue Hospital, Tim and Gus had been called to Connecticut for an emergency meeting of the *End The War Committee* and Ray and Suzanne had gone up to the Farm and had not, as yet, returned. Miss Bean relayed all this in her usual brisk manner while standing in the hallway of the Kenmare Street apartments. About Mercedes, she said not to worry, she actually looked the picture of health, her slight fever giving her a ruddy glow. Jonathan wondered just what kind of nurse Miss Bean had been, but she was probably right about Mercedes and it was his nature to worry. He knew that.

When he saw Mercedes the next morning, she did look healthy in the flushed way Miss Bean had described, but her speech was slurred. "It's like my tongue is drunk. Think I caught it from Arty?"

He resisted any note of alarm creeping into his voice. "I dunno. Are you feeling an urge to throw bricks?"

Mercedes laughed but it was a peculiar laugh, strangled and slightly guttural. He frowned and caught a look in her eye.

"So, what's going on?"

"They don't know."

Later that afternoon while Jonathan was still at Bellevue, Tim and Gus returned to the House. Del was helping Ed prepare the evening meal and noted how Gus immediately huffed over to the side bench and sat down next to Scotty who was dozing, his head tucked into the collar of his greatcoat with only a tousle of wispy, white hair announcing a human presence. She noticed how Gus pulled out his pipe, filled it, tamped it, lit it and hid behind a curtain of smoke. His face had an iodine-red glow. She heard Tim say the word "Trotskyites" to Ed who stood over by the coffee urn.

"Trotskyites" was a word that always stopped Del in her tracks. What were they anyway? When she finally met one, he was just a skinny, pallid-faced kid from City College who talked fast in a spray of spittle. Gus referenced them as though they were the scourge of the peace movement while Tim, who felt most discussions regarding factionalism were best settled by lifting an ale at McSorley's, laughed them off. There had been some disagreement, some trouble Tim was saying. But the event was still on and November 6th was to be the day.

It would all move swiftly now, they knew. Whatever was to happen.

— 30 —

Dreams

That night after Jonathan left, Mercedes had dreams of
Africa. Drums and people calling to one another that
someone had died. The village was being informed.
The sheets were hot. The water put to her lips tasted
of tin. Shoes on the linoleum floor sounded like the
scurrying of rats. Somewhere a light flashed like heat
lightning over the lake. There was a mumbling incanta-
tion over her bed. Someone put a cool shell to her chest.
Words sounded far off and ancient, a language she knew
nothing about. She wanted her own bed. Where was
her own bed? In the morning, as gray light filtered
through the venetian blinds, she discovered she could
not speak.

Once when she was ten or eleven, before her parents
gave up their attempt at small farming and moved to
San Francisco, she went with her father to a farm in
Sonoma because he was going to buy a beef calf for
their small ranch. The year before he had gotten a

milk cow but he wasn't able to breed her successfully and he wanted to raise a calf for slaughter. Mercedes went along to see the new calf.

It was black and white with knobby knees and still stanchioned alongside its mother. The farmer was a tall man with white hair and blue overalls. He spoke kindly in low tones to the mother cow and held her pressed against her side of the pen with his body while Mercedes' father put a rope around the calf's neck and pulled him toward the gate. The mother cow twisted her head violently to see her calf and the farmer grunted and leaned against her more heavily. Mercedes thought she had never seen such wild eyes. Human, frantic, wild eyes. As she and her father got back into the truck with the trailer and the calf inside, she kept hearing the mother cow bawl and bawl.

She thought about this now as she felt her own eyes widen and upon opening her mouth, heard a stricken sound.

— 31 —

Louie The Hat

Louie told Del she looked terrible. Terrible for someone so young. She should go out and have a good time.
Louie was a sign painter, the last of a dying breed although Del didn't know that in 1965. In 1965, Louie's
shop was down the street from Saint Jude's and where
Del went once a week to get away from the House and
earn some cash.

"It's not a pearl, Della Del. Not a pearl. Come here.
Leave that alone. Sit down." Louie whisked debris off
a low stool beside his chair. He was carefully applying
shellac to a piece of oak, dipping the brush just so,
making the stroke smooth. A perfectionist. His shop
could go to hell but his craft was impeccable.

Del was picking up strips of vinyl molding that had
been kicked under a table. She was mumbling about
Joaquin and Nester.

"Don't bother," said Louie. "Look. The boys come
in and they go. They do the plastics. They make a

mess but they pay the rent. No one wants hand-painted anymore." He looked over at Del again and patted the stool. "I got the shop, a few regulars but the boys pay the rent. So what? They got *The Chicken America* job. You think you're so smart, Del, huh? So smart. Chicken America, Spaghetti America, Turnip America. So smart. It's a good country. What it do to you?"

Del was trying to straighten up the place but it was hopeless. Everywhere she turned she either stepped on vinyl clippings or saw something else kicked under one of the two, twelve-foot-long tables dominating the space.

"Don't. Don't sweep. The dust will stick." The tabletops were usually littered. The boys' table had either on or under it aluminum edging, plastic, fabricated letters, metal sheers, clippers, ladders, sweatshirts, bottles of coke and cerveza. The boys were Joaquin Arce and Nester Rodriguez, both married men. They were noisy and mouthy and harmless and got under your skin with their constant music and girlie talk. Del shrugged and scanned Louie's particular disaster. Every flat surface except his upright drafting table was strewn with sheets of brown wrapping paper, tubes of half-squeezed oils, varnish, linseed oil, stained rags, shellac, brushes soaking in bottles, crumpled butcher's paper smudged with mustard and flecks of pastrami, copies of the Daily News, cream soda. An aluminum extension ladder and busted up framing for signs were stashed underneath another long table to the rear. Also under that table could be found Louie's salvaged political work: Nelson Rockefeller grinning with a mustache. Bella with a black eye. Lindsey with some teeth blacked out.

"Della, they gotta have a job too. Huh? Huh?" He was still defending, "the boys". Del looked at him blowing lightly over the newly applied shellac and then blocking out letters in mime tracing with his hand in front of the wood. She came and sat down on the stool. Louie smiled.

"So, here I put the doctor's name, underneath that, his specialty, feet, elbows, what you got, the address, the phone number. The doctor symbol, I pounce in over here, to the right, those snakes and things. Why you look like that? You don't like doctors either? Lawyers you don't like. Politicians you don't like. Doctors too? God forbid you fall down or eat the wrong thing late at night. What do you do then? The lawyer. The politician. I can understand. But, the doctors. If they save my life, who cares how much they make? Forget it. Look." He reached out and took out several clean brushes from their glass jar.

"I want to show you something. This is what is important here, Della Del. First, the brushes. Camel hair, the finest. Soft, won't scratch the leaf. Bristle brushes are too stiff. Feel that. Go on. Feel." She felt the tip of one of the larger brushes. She felt the tip of one of the smaller brushes.

"Like silk." Del said. Louie glanced over to check if

she were being a smart aleck. He hardly had any eyebrows, only sparse hairs poking out from above puffy lids and tiny, watery, pinprick eyes. He had a pointy nose, small, moist lips and a pink tongue, the tip of which he bit while concentrating.

"This, you make sure is clean." He stroked the hairs of one of the larger brushes. "This must be free from dirt. Don't laugh. Why? So, the place is messy. I told you, it's not a pearl. But, this, right here, here are the jewels. Even this." He tapped the metal heel of the brush where the hairs were attached. "Even this. It's important. Clean. No "foreign" particles. That I hope's not against your politics?" He winked.

"So, that's what needs to be clean. The rest, we forget. The boys, we leave alone. Tonight, we let this dry. Tomorrow we do the sizing, then we pounce, then the gold. Takes time."

It was late afternoon. Sun, full and sharp, streamed in through the grimy picture window overlooking Chrystie Street. Dust motes skittered. Del found herself staring at the jar of linseed oil sitting on a ledge next to Louie's drafting table. "Fat oil" he called it, the oil two-toned with a sludgy yellow gunk settling at the bottom and pale yellow syrup surfacing to the top. It made Del wonder about cream rising? Why did it do that? Why didn't it sink like fat oil?

"Hey, Della Del, you in a trance? You're too much. Too much with the bums. With the war. You think you can make it different?" Louie had gotten up and pecked his way to the rear of the shop where he propped the shellacked sign against the wall having cleared a space on the long table. He was sighing, shaking his head.

"Go run to Katz's. Get me pastrami, lots of spicy and a pickle. Sauerkraut, too. Go on. Get something for yourself. Something good. Cream soda, too. You don't like? Get a coke. Here. Don't bring back. Keep the change. Hurry." Louie pressed a ten-dollar bill into Del's hand and she was out the door.

This made sense. This errand for Louie. She would walk over there and order two pastrami sandwiches. She would stop at the corner and look both ways and not have any stupid thoughts about walking into traffic. She wouldn't think about the war or the draft or the FBI or the wiretaps or jail or Mercedes being moved to Intensive Care or the boyfriend she had just broken up with. She would be a normal person.

When Del returned, pastrami sandwiches in hand, Louie immediately pushed away from his work and cleared a space amid the tracing paper he was using to map out a template. She watched him unwrap the white butcher paper and pat it flat upon his lap. He made little cooing sounds to his sandwich and remarked on the size and firmness of the pickle, the briny ooze and peppercorns stuck to the paper.

"This is good. Look at this here." Louie held up half his sandwich, a great slab of pastrami threatening to slide, skidding on a layer of sauerkraut and mustard. "Where's yours, Del?" She held up her bag.

"Good. You eat it. Meat. You need that. What you eat over there? Loaves and fishes?" He laughed at that. They both did.

— 32 —

Louie's Thoughts

Della Del. Della Del. Crazy with the war, with the bums, that's what Louie thought. She looked like a refugee there with that green dress, all faded and the elbows pokin' through. Not that she should look like a floozy but a little rouge on her cheek would be nice. Dark circles under her eyes. No good. No good. No parties. No dances. All demonstrations. Here. There. This and that. Getting arrested. Stupid. What good would it do?

A girl should have some nice things, go to dances. Not that he ever did at that age. Too shy. Too much work. Work. Work. But for him, he had to. Him, he had reason. His mother, her hands, the arthritis even then and his father dead. But, Del? No. A good home, food, parents. What she do that for? Get arrested and not tell her parents.

Crazy. He shook his head and straightened his back from leaning over the table. He swished the brush in

a milky swirl of turpentine. He wiped the tip clean
and put the cool hairs to his cheek. So nice, it felt.
So smooth. Like a girl's wrist, he imagined, not that
he knew a lot about that either. At least she had the
boyfriend, the one she was always getting rid of. Not
that Louie didn't understand that. He was a nice kid
but forgets. Says he'll do and then forgets. Louie suspected it was the herbs. For Louie? Never. Camels or
Lucky Strikes, of course. He whisked off the square of
table before him, made everything nice for tomorrow.
He shrugged on his coat, patted and adjusted the hat
that never left his head and then squinting into the afternoon light stood quietly for a few moments before
the window.

— 33 —

Del's Thoughts

Louie had kept looking at her today and shaking his head. He'd shake and then bite the pink tip of his tongue. He was concentrating on the Abramowitz Jewelers job. It had a line drawing of a woman's hand with a diamond ring featured on her stylistically elongated and arched ring finger. He had been struggling to get the facets right all day. Finally, it was as he wished and now he was doing the border. He would look at Del out of the corner of his eye, scowl and then, biting the tip of his tongue, rest his drawing hand on the raised wrist of the other hand steadying himself as he articulated a clean, bold, black border. He'd frown, shake his head, beetle his brow, look sideways again.

They had argued about the war and about the boys and their doing *The Chicken America* work. He didn't know why Del couldn't shut up about it. The war he felt was what people did. Their nature. The big guys grab; the little guys pay. Not if you don't give them the money, she'd say. There she goes, he'd say. The tax refusal, the draft refusal. Who makes sure the streets are paved and we don't fall into a big hole, he'd say. Not all is for the bombs.

She'd started to say something to him and then stopped. Then he said, "Go to Katz's." And so she did and they ended up on a good note. Now Del had her pastrami sandwich to take back to the apartment. She had eaten half with Louie and saved the rest for later. She wanted a little something to eat before she went out that evening. Tonight she and Jonathan were going to the San Gennaro Festival.

— 34 —

Festa di San Gennaro

Jonathan said he'd meet her on the corner of Mulberry and Broome. Walking to meet him, Del stopped to eye a coil of sausage the guy behind a grill on Mulberry was searing while rhapsodizing on its anatomical possibilities. It made her blush even though she only guessed the references. His hand gestures were explicit. As she turned to move on down the street, she caught sight of Jonathan leaning against a light post. He was tall and slender and the most handsome boy she had ever known. He moved through the crowd and stretched out his hand. "Let's walk."

She had never held hands with Jonathan, but his invitation was casual and her response automatic. Besides, with the crush of people on the street, the yelling, the music, the dazzle of lights, the booths and the Ferris wheel making its improbable arc over the tenements, it was a natural and sensible thing to do. They shouldered and jostled their way up Mulberry. They stared at the bubbling vats of lard where dough was flung, submerged and then bobbed up golden to be later dusted with confectioner's sugar. They threw hoops over bottles and Jonathan won a fuzzy, little, blue duck and gave it to her. They slipped into the church to check out the statue of San Gennaro bedecked with lights and pinned-on paper money and after a few irreverent remarks ran out of the garish gloom and down onto the street. They lingered in front of a booth selling candies and Jonathan bought two little boxes of Torrone. Del had never tasted the candy before and biting into one she told Jonathan it felt as if she were receiving communion. The papery exterior stuck to her lower lip but then the frothy mix of nuts and honey assured her she was communing with a far different sensation. They both stood on the sidewalk in a trance of chewing. Del felt happy. She was aware they were not talking about Saint Jude's or the war or Mercedes or Tim or any of it. It was more like they were on a date. Jonathan must have picked up on the mood because he made some comment about how even Jesus partied now and then. By now, they were on the outskirts of the festival on Broadway. They cut over onto East Houston skirting the fringes of the festival. They had stopped holding hands although Jonathan had taken off his sweater and draped it over Del's shoulders and with mock-gallantry had fastened the sleeves loosely under her chin. They walked in silence down Elizabeth to the corner of Kenmare. The festival was still going strong one block west but it was almost one in the morning and Del was feeling tired and a bit awkward. They mounted the outside steps to Kenmare Street and Jonathan pushed open the front door, the sleeve of his shirt brushing her cheek. They walked up the one flight and stood outside the women's apartment. Light from inside leaked under the door jamb and Jonathan inquired if Mother Sadie were waiting up. Del laughed and said she didn't think so. More likely, Sadie had left the light on to confuse the cockroaches since she hated them more than anything. Del fiddled with the cuffs of Jonathan's sweater and said she'd had a great time. She untwisted the loose knot around her neck and let the sweater fall over her right arm. He said, "I did too." They both said, "Thanks," their words colliding and they laughed.

Jonathan took the sweater and put it on, shrugging his shoulders and tugging the sleeves up to his elbows. They were standing close and he reached out and pulled Del toward him. They kissed. One kiss. Del didn't pull away. She lingered. His lips were very soft. Then she pressed her cheek against his chest and heard the quick, strong beat of his heart. "So, can I have another date?" he said. And Del said foolishly, flippantly, "Sure, jump on the merry-go-round."

She was nervous that Tim might come up or down the stairs and discover them both there together. She pulled away noticing how Jonathan's lips pursed and bowed up at the corners. His wary smile. She thanked him again for the evening and entered her apartment, closing the door behind her, listening to his footsteps going back down the stairs and not up.

35

Next Week

Jonathan finally coaxed Del into visiting Mercedes. The clincher was when he said, "She's been in there for almost two weeks and you haven't gone once." This was true. The fact was, Del was scared. Both Jonathan and Tim had confirmed that Mercedes was in bad shape. She had recently been moved into Intensive Care having totally lost the power of speech. She could make guttural sounds and move her head up, down and sideways, but her legs were paralyzed and the cause remained a mystery. Jonathan maintained an upbeat agitation about the situation, going to see her every evening and, if he could not make an evening, popping in during the afternoon. In the beginning Mercedes had not wished her mother told. But, this current turn was frightening and had everyone at Saint Jude's wondering what the best course of action should be.

Miss Day had been notified at the Farm and was planning to return to the city. What could a person do that was not already being done? It was a terrible love that drove people to do this work. This is what she thought and sometimes a terrible love demanded sacrifices we could not foresee or understand. Still, she felt the mother should know.

That evening both Jonathan and Del stood alongside Mercedes' hospital bed with the side panels pulled up. She lay on her back with her torso slightly elevated, her head raised. She had foam wedges placed alongside her legs and between her knees and pillows positioned on either side of her hips. She looked oddly radiant, feverish maybe, and smiled when they entered and looked happy when Jonathan leaned over and gave her a quick kiss on the lips and then rocked back lightly on his heels saying, "Ummm, milk of magnesia." She laughed in her strangled way and Del noticed as Jonathan rocked back that Mercedes had a chalky smudge over her upper lip. Del stepped to the side of the bed and squeezed Mercedes' hand. It was limp and hot and she wanted to pull away as much from that sensation as from the look on Mercedes' face.

A nurse bustled in with a paper cup of pills and a glass of water with a straw. She administered the medicine and took Mercedes' temperature, noting what was done on the chart; then, adjusting the wedges and pillows, left. When the door was shut, Jonathan lifted the chart from the end of the bed and flipped expertly to the last page. He leaned over Mercedes conspiratorially and said the nurse wrote that, "The patient appears intoxicated by the rapturous attentions of the young man by her side." Amazing, Del thought. They are still doing this coquettish, little dance. What was she, the chaperone? Then, she felt small and mean-spirited. Mercedes was making the same strangled noises and rolling her head from side to side. Del thought it grotesque. Jonathan turned nonchalantly through a few more pages and then with a flourish re-attached the chart to its proper place. He continued talking non-stop filling Mercedes in on various House activities and the plans for the upcoming demonstration while Del looked everywhere but at the woman in the bed. She fixated on the machines measuring heartbeat, respiration, blood pressure, the squiggly lines, the numbers changing. Every so often Mercedes' left leg would spasm and Jonathan's hand would immediately go there, holding the leg steady, stroking and calming it as one would an unruly child. Del thought, he's done this before. He glanced over at Del and she, at least, had the presence of mind to tell a funny Sadie story that she thought Mercedes might enjoy, but Del wanted out of there. Another nurse knocked and entering asked them if they would please leave for a few minutes since she needed to attend to a personal matter. Jonathan nodded and said, "See you in a bit," and they both left the room. Exiting, he walked swiftly past the nurses' station, through the visitors' waiting room and into the corridor where he slammed his fist against the cement wall alongside the elevator doors. He had read in the chart, "Cramps in calf muscles continuing, headache, nausea, restlessness, ataxia, and progressive paralysis of legs and arms."

36

The Men's Apartment, Sunday Morning

Tim was reading *The Sunday New York Times.* He
had the front pages creased lengthwise and propped up
against a stack of books on the kitchen table in the
men's apartment. He made a long, low whistle. "God
almighty, look at this. Front page. ***Quaker Burns
Himself To Death In Front of Pentagon.***"

Gus was sitting on top of the enamel tub-top scowling and tamping tobacco into his pipe and Ray was
looking inside the refrigerator trying to find something
to eat.

"Listen. *Norman Morrison, a 32 year old Quaker
from Baltimore, burned himself to death in front of the
Pentagon in an anti-war protest yesterday.* Poor bastard."

Ray closed the refrigerator door, a jar of grape jelly
in his hand. Gus struck a match and looked at the
plume of flame as he sucked it down and into the bowl
of his pipe. He coughed a few times.

119

Tim whistled low again. "Next headline. ***391 Vietcong Killed in All-Day Battle Near Saigon.*** Near Saigon. Isn't that supposed to be 'our territory'? And, here's another from the, Oops, Sorry 'Bout That Department, ***Second Vietnam Town Bombed In Error***. He smacked another crease in the paper and looking up continued, "But, don't worry, Gentle Reader. It says here that only 48 people were killed and that the mistake was caused by a South Vietnamese First Lieutenant who's going to be court-marshaled. Bet that will be a real democratic process carried out on a Saigon street."

Ray was spreading grape jelly idly on a slice of bread and shaking his head while Gus was wreathed in a cloud of smoke and silence.

"Now, on the home front." Tim was on a roll. "***Negroes Still Angry and Jobless Three Months After Watts Riot***. I say, whatever is their problem?"

Gus cleared his throat. "Anything in there about us?" He was getting impatient with Tim's editorializing. In truth, he was surprised the nitwit could even read.

"I'm looking. I'm looking." Gus could see that the paper was now creased at the Sports Section. He could see a beefy thigh kicking out to the edge of a folded page. He knew Tim was doing this to annoy him. Tim flipped the pages back to a middle section. "Ok. Local news. Let's see if that guy they sent got it right. Here we go."

End-War Group Near Break-Up Over Strat-

egy. Tim snorted, "Whoa, there's a catchy headline that falls trippingly from the tongue. Maybe this story should be in the Society Pages."

"Just read it, Tim," said Gus. The room was filling up with annoyed puffs of smoke and Ray was laughing while spreading jam on another slice of bread.

Tim cleared his throat and shot Ray an amused look. "Ok," he said, "Here we go."

"Tension among some segments of the anti-war movement here became apparent last week when the New York Committee to End the War in Vietnam threatened to disband. Sources within the Committee said that one of the major reasons was a strategic difference between representatives of the Trotskyite Socialist Worker's Party and members of the Students for a Democratic Society."

Gus grunted. "But, is there anything in there about us? About the planned draft card burning?" Gus was now standing in front of the tub. Tim was scanning the article and paraphrasing. It says the composition of the group ranges from traditional, pacifist groups to members of the new student left to older radical groups which, oh, here's a nice phrase, 'have in the past been bitterly sectarian.' Blah, blah, blah and then this bit about how the Trots were interested in what they are calling 'minimum slogans' raising only the single issue of ending the war while the SDS kids want to build a broader coalition for social change and are calling the Trots doctrinaire. Oh, man. Then that SDS kid from

Columbia (he'll probably run for the US Senate in a few years) is quoted as saying that, 'There's a great deal of friction in trying to blah, blah, blah and it's a problem of strategy'.

"So, to answer your question, Gus. No. No mention of us or of the planned draft card burning."

Gus had taken out another pipe. Ray was pacing from the refrigerator to the kitchen table and back again prompting Tim to have the ghoulish thought that this was probably good practice for what Ray would probably be doing a lot of for the next three to five years.

"Fuck 'em," said Ray. "We'll do it as planned."

— 37 —

After Compline

Dorothy Day had returned to the House from the Farm in the early evening and now after saying Compline had retired to her room at Saint Jude's taking with her a cup of tea and some toast. She was weary. She had called Mercedes' mother and assured her that her daughter was being taken care of and how it had been Mercedes' wish not to worry her but Dorothy felt she should know. Mrs. McCann was grateful and said she would make arrangements to travel East. Dorothy offered lodgings in the women's apartment where Mercedes had slept but there was a distinct silence on the other end of the line and then a, "Thank you. I'll be in touch after I've seen my daughter."

This was not something Dorothy ordinarily did, call the parents of the young people who came to work at Saint Jude's. But, the passage in the Bible where Jesus admonished his Mother, *I must be about my Father's work* always tore at her heart. A mother's worry does

123

not cease because a child is doing good. A mother needs to know. She said a prayer and hoped she had done the right thing. Closing her eyes, she felt agitated as well as weary. She remembered the time when Graham was restless beyond repair that last summer when they rented the cottage on Staten Island, how he would get a bottle of Olde English Furniture Oil and set to polishing all the wooden furniture in the cottage. The rocker, the gate-leg table, the beautifully scrolled bookcase they brought with them from the apartment on Spring Street. Even Cara's crib although she had forbade him to put any oil on the chewed surface of the side-gates where their daughter gnawed like a little beaver. He would put records on the phonograph and rub to the measure of the music. This would calm him, calm him away from the horrors of what he saw as the constant blunderings of man-made institutions, the economic inequities built into those institutions, the horrible, horrible waste of life as when Sacco and Vanzetti were executed, an event from which she thought Graham had never fully recovered. That and her conversion to Catholicism.

Her own room at Saint Jude's was reminiscent of that cottage, a hugger-mugger comfortableness about it, her bed, her chairs, her desk. She was now sitting in one of the two well-worn, stuffed chairs that sat facing one another with a shaded lamp alongside her chair casting a halo of yellow light. The bookcase, the books and her desk were all of the possessions remaining of that past life. They brought back that time, the salt tang still in their pores. It had been a happy time for her, almost bovine with happiness. And, with that, yes, the guilt.

Friends escaping the city for a respite from their political work would chide Dorothy and Graham between mouthfuls of the clams Graham had brought in and washed and steamed and served to them with butter and thick slices of bread. She and Graham belonged on the picket line with them, they would say, not here, not retreating during these worst of times. She would argue and debate but Graham would grow silent. The next morning, he would take off, not saying goodbye to the overnight guests, rowing his dory into the early morning fog, staying all day, coming in only at sunset with crabs he'd throw into the sink with no words other than they'd need to be steamed that evening.

Reflexively, she reached out and stroked the side of the bookcase next to her chair, its surface so smooth, a comfort. She thought of the sculptor, Henry Moore, whose biography she was currently reading. The image came to her of Moore as a child rubbing liniment into his mother's back. She saw in her mind's eye the massive backs Moore sculpted, so obsidian, so remotely smooth and she stroked the side of the bookcase again. Old friend. It served two functions, holding her books, her other dear friends and, now, giving her this comfort, this slow, languorous motion of her hand.

— 38 —

Augustus

It was late but Gus could see from under Dorothy's
door that the light was still on. He tapped lightly. He
paused. He wouldn't knock again. He had already
decided that. But, her voice said, "Come in." Opening
the door, he stood there feeling foolish, tugging on his
ear, clearing his throat, thinking, Say it.

"Dorothy, I know it's late in the evening but may I
have a moment of your time before you retire?"

She felt vexed, resigned. He was so formal, she
thought. So, old world. Really, more like her father
than a man nearly forty years her junior. She motioned
him in gesturing to the chair opposite hers.

God, he thought, she has a look that could shrivel
your scrotum. But then the look softened as he sat and
inquired if he might smoke his pipe. She nodded. Gus
cleared his throat again. "I've just come from Lafayette
Street. Tim and Ray came late and are still there." She
studied him as he prepared his pipe, lit it and took two

lengthy draws.

"Five of us are prepared to burn our draft cards this Saturday. Ray, Tim, myself, Cliff MacDaniels from WIN and a young student named Billy Watson from Brooklyn College. I'm a little concerned about him. He just dropped out of school last week and still has his student deferment. I don't think he's thought the whole thing through. He's nineteen."

Dorothy had long given up cautioning youth to be prudent. She would pray but she knew that offering would be of little comfort to the man sitting before her. But, Gus had already moved on to another topic.

"They want me to invite you to speak at the rally."

This was such a simple request that Dorothy was perplexed as to why Augustus felt it so difficult to ask. Surely, he knew her answer.

"I don't think you should," he said. "I know you would want to but I have grave doubts about security. And there have been threats. MacDaniels and WIN received this the other day. I asked if I could show it to you."

Gus leaned forward, pulled a small envelope from his rear pocket, and handed it to Dorothy. It was smudged and wrinkled, the mailing address penciled in childish letters that slanted upwards towards the right corner. She opened the envelope and took out a single sheet of torn copybook paper.

"Basturds, commie skum, Don't think We don't no you. Die and fry, draft dodger queer pinko skum."

Dorothy smiled and folded up the lined paper, sliding it back into the envelope. She handed it back to Gus.

"Ran out of steam at the end, don't you think—repeating 'skum' twice?" Dorothy had seen so many of these letters, so many of those poor, misshapen words. Seen them and heard them and had them spit at her.

Gus shifted his weight forward in the chair and frowned, "I really don't think you should speak, Miss Day. WIN's offices were broken into last week and the mimeo machine was beaten with a hammer or wrench or something and drawers were tossed and the mailing lists stolen. The phone is tapped." Dorothy was smiling again. "I know, it's tapped here too," he said. Gus was getting red in the face, realizing the futility of his cautions.

"Well, we do have a permit. And, the police have assured us that they would provide adequate protection." The fox guarding the hen house is what Dorothy thought about that. She fingered the book on her lap and patted its cover. "Tell them I'd be honored to speak at the rally, Augustus. Let them know I won't have a long speech. Tell me when it is best to arrive and Miss Bean and I will take the subway up to Union Square."

Gus rubbed his eyes and face and tapped the spent tobacco from his pipe into the palm of his hand. Dorothy passed him the saucer under her cup. She noticed he had the hands of a stone mason, stubby and thick.

A worker-scholar's hands. She said this and he smiled at the flattery, standing up resignedly, a man who had honorably discharged his duty to a predictable but troubling outcome. He inched his pipe into the side pocket of his work pants while motioning her to remain seated. He was a small man, maybe five feet six or seven, who gave the impression of height by his solid frame and erect posture. Dorothy thought, given his nature, this lack of height must have been a trial but she knew it would prepare him for adversity if not endearments.

"Well," he mused, "I supposed I would fail in my mission but I felt I had to at least try to let you know how I perceived the situation." Dorothy thanked him for his concern but said in her experience she found that such threats generally exhausted the writer through the sheer effort it took to grasp a pencil and form the misshapen words. She wasn't worried. Gus shook his head and after patting his pockets automatically for his pipe and pouch said goodnight and let himself out the door. After he left, Dorothy clicked off the lamp and sat in the dark suddenly sickened by both the impoverished letter and her clever tongue.

— 39 —

The Bent World

Jonathan had spent an entire day at the Columbia Medical Library looking through books on multiple sclerosis and other diseases of the central nervous system. He had taken out several volumes on tropical diseases with horribly graphic photographs of illness and disfigurement. He was searching for any of the words he saw on the medical chart at the foot of Mercedes' bed. He was trying to piece together some understanding from the eavesdropped conversations and direct discussions he had had with several of her doctors who viewed him as a possible conduit between Mercedes and her family. He had kept faith with her request not to notify her mother but he understood why Miss Day had felt impelled to call California with the news. All the blood work, the brain scans, the neurological tests were inconclusive. Simply, her worsening condition remained a mystery. They were now working on the theory that it was some strange virus or parasite and had called in a specialist with expertise in topical diseases, but to date, no one could match her symptoms with a cause. Lacking that, what they were doing was merely keeping her comfortable and watching as the fevers came and went and the paralysis progressed. On more than one occasion, Jonathan slammed a book shut raising eyebrows of others in the reading room.

He could behave like a frenzied man when danger threatened his loved ones. He had been that way when his brother Ted went through the ice. Even though he was a kid, he went back to where Ted had fallen through and with a splitting-maul angrily broke a wide hole around the parameter of the weak ice so that it would be observable and no one else would fall through. It was a silly act and dangerous but it made him feel better. Then, last month when Del was bitten by a spider and had an allergic reaction, he emptied a whole can of Raid into the women's apartment. But, this thing with Mercedes left him feeling dangerously helpless. Neither a can of Raid or a splitting-maul was of the remotest use.

*

Mercedes knew Jonathan had been there but when? Today? Yesterday? Morning? Evening? He had read from Hopkins, the poem she loved, the one that ended with,

132

Because the Holy Ghost over the bent
  World broods with warm breast and with ah! bright wings.

But, she was bent. She didn't know what was happening. She was back in Tanzania, somewhere near Lake Victoria. Maybe it was Musoma and she was practicing her first words of Swahili. She was in the marketplace and had asked for a *lifti* and the woman gave her an onion. She thought, My God, I can speak and be understood. But, I can't. I can't speak. What is this? Someone help me. The nurses' feet go in and out, their crepe shoes like the squeak of rats.

— 40 —

Late Night Thoughts

Dorothy Day was not immune from worry over her physical safety. The images of the WIN office machinery being hammered, the rooms vandalized, the phones tapped, the threats, all of it so predictable were still, especially in late night, quiet moments, unsettling.

She did not like violence–either seeing it or hearing it or having it visited upon her person. She still heard Ella's screams from the forced feedings in the DC jail, still felt the bites of gravel in her knee and cheek as she fell running from the mounted police in Washington Square Park. She still heard the taunts. But, she would speak. It was a matter of conscience and continuing on and not forgetting.

She clicked the light on again and opened up the current book on her lap and continued reading. The narrator was quoting Sophocles, *Who is the slayer, who the victim? Speak.* What prompted those ancient lines? Some other endless war and now this new one nipping

133

at their heels and young men again being sacrificed. And, soon, the very ones here in the soup kitchen off to jail, to that other battlefield. How could she not speak?

She wanted sleep but was too tired to sleep. All around her New York City teemed. A siren in the disance. Someone walking by her window, calling out.

She knew she would hear all the old words. *Go Back To Russia. Pinko. Commie. Better Dead Than Red.*

Now there was only the hiss of tires down the street, a garbage can falling over, the yowl of a cat. It was one in the morning by the clock's illuminated dial. A restless city in a restless night. She closed her eyes and remembered the words of that evening's Compline, *Because the poor are oppressed. Because the poor are exploited. I will rise up now sayeth the Lord.* She thought of her Communist Party friends who said religion was the opiate of the people. It had not put her to sleep. She could use some opiate tonight but religion was not it.

— 41 —

Getting Ready For The Day

The day of the draft card burning dawned cool and bright. The streets had a washed and glittery feel to them and Del woke early. She had heard Tim go down the stairs about twenty minutes ago and knew both he and Gus were part of a committee going to Union Square at seven to meet with the police and discuss security. Authorities had assured the organizers that there would be plain-clothes as well as uniformed officers monitoring the crowd. Gus told Tim that he also wanted to double-check that one "of our own people" would be close to Dorothy Day at all times. Tim thought Gus's concern for Dorothy patronizing. His relationship with her was much less reverential. He didn't talk the big ideas with her but more the mundane matters of the House. How many pounds of potatoes or crates of kohlrabi should he pick up at the Fulton Fish Market? Could the beat-up Chevy with its rear seat removed so they could haul donated clothing and produce

135

last another winter? What to do about Arty when he went on a toot? Tim wasn't one to sit at the hem of her skirt and listen to parables. He stayed when she was talking labor history and Debs and Emma Goldman and Joe Hill and the IWW, but if the subject turned religious, he made his excuses. Gus, on the other hand, listened to it all and treated Dorothy with deference. Tim thought of her more as an older, feisty colleague who could tell one hell of a story. But, he didn't mention any of this to Gus as they walked up to 14th Street and Union Square. Ray had told them not to bother picking him up. He said he would walk up later with Suzanne and Del.

Jonathan was still half-asleep when Tim left the apartment. He had gone out with everyone last night at Tim's invitation "to lift a few" and was still groggy. He wasn't a big drinker but felt glad to be included. It felt good to be standing there at the bar and talking about tomorrow's demonstration. Hanging out like he belonged. Edmund also dropped by for a quick beer before heading home to Spring Street. He and Jonathan spoke a little about Mercedes since Ed was also a regular visitor. They both fell silent after a few words on the subject. Mercedes' mother had arrived and was staying in a reasonably priced mid-town hotel having politely declined Dorothy's offer of lodging. Mrs. McCann and Edmund had met with some rapport but she looked suspiciously at Jonathan.

Actually, Jonathan also felt rapport with Ed, even

though he was older. Ed's having attempted monastery life was one reason but, more importantly, it was his genuine kindness and solidity. He had been at Saint Jude's longer than any other volunteer and in Jonathan's estimation seemed the most content. Saint Jude's was his vocation, freely chosen, a life of meager means embraced fully and with a happy heart.

They talked while Tim and Ray were drinking shooters of applejack and bantering with Gus (who dismissed applejack as "Yankee moonshine") and then the three of them started debating which drinks were proletarian and which were ruling class. It all seemed good-natured, but why risk even a good-natured, ideological snit when tomorrow could mean anyone of them being trotted off to jail. Maybe with this in mind, they all had the good sense to end the evening on an early note.

Jonathan rubbed his eyes and stretched, rolled out of bed, pulled on his jeans and shirt and sweater. He threw cold water on his face, brushed his teeth, ran fingers through his hair and was out the door.

When Del arrived at Ray and Suzanne's apartment at eight, only Suzanne was there. Ray had changed his mind and already gone up to Union Square saying he was too nervous to wait around. Suzanne's eyes were red.

"He hardly slept a wink last night," she said. "He kept getting up. I'd hear him in the kitchen mumbling to himself, going over his statement. When I went in to check, he told me to go back to bed. I made him nervous."

Apart from being red-eyed and pregnant, Suzanne looked chic in a new, emerald green, corduroy maternity outfit Ray's mother had bought for her. Del slipped off her jacket and tossed it onto one of the kitchen chairs, showing off her own stylish, clothing-room find, a *Peck & Peck*, burnt-umber shirtwaist with matching belt. They shared their standard gambit about sacrifices they made for the revolution. Suzanne thought Del still smarted at the newspaper report claiming they looked like a bunch of "shabby peaceniks" when they were arrested for blocking the doors of the Whitehall Street Induction Center. Del had to admit, the article did rankle, especially since they had tried so hard to look respectable, the guys wearing suits with slicked hair and the girls in nylons.

Suzanne placed two coffee cups on the table and plugged in the electric percolator, a wonderfully out-of-sync wedding gift that brewed a rich Medaglio D'Oro. They sat in silence listening to the pot burble and hiss and then Suzanne poured a black stream from its swan-like beak and cut slices of warmed Babka from Odessa's.

"Ray looked great," she said. "He's wearing that suit he bought for Dewey's sentencing. He thinks it's poetic justice since he'll be committing civil disobedience in clothing that once witnessed an act of subjugation. He talks like that all the time now. I'll be so happy when this day is over." Del agreed saying how she'd be happy, too, when things got back to normal. Suzanne paused over her coffee cup, looking up at Del with raised eyebrows. "Yeah. Normal."

They both laughed, put the dishes in the sink, slipped on their jackets, checked the stove, locked the door and headed uptown.

— 42 —

Union Square

Union Square had been the launching site in 1933 for The Catholic Worker Movement. It was there on May Day, the workers' holiday, where the first copies of ***The Agitator*** were given away to the unemployed sitting on park benches. Four months later, the movement boasted a monthly run of 25,000 and today it was still strong.

On some weekends Tim and Del would go up to the square to hawk papers. Tim was particularly good at it and would call out catchy phrases like, "Only a penny a copy. Afflict the comfortable. Comfort the afflicted. Read ***The Agitator***." If they had a prosperous afternoon, they would then go and spend some of their profits in Chinatown. This seemed vaguely larcenous to Del but not so much that she'd forgo a good meal. Sometimes Tim would hawk the paper solo in spots like Times Square or Rockefeller Center and come home with his pockets stuffed with bills. Slapping down his earnings like poker winnings on the kitchen table in the men's apartment, he'd grin, "Guilt pays". Then, they'd really hit Chinatown and have roast duck with enough money left over for some good Irish tobacco or high quality cigars.

Turning right on Fourteenth Street off Fifth Avenue, Del and Suzanne saw double police barricades already positioned and the paddy wagons lined up over by Kline's Department Store. A sizeable number of counter-demonstrators were already assembled and cordoned off on the west corner of Union Square, waving the usual **Better Dead Than Red** and **Go Back To Russia** signs. The rally staging could be seen through the trees in the middle of the square. Entering through a break in one of the barricades, they threaded their way through an already growing crowd. Voices shouted over to the right as police officers materialized and escorted a rumpled, middle-aged man in a brown suit with a blown-up replica of a draft card pinned to his jacket and holding an *I FOUGHT MY WAR* sign.

"I seen you guys. I seen you guys before," he was yelling looking backwards at two college students in army surplus jackets carrying stacks of *Progressive Labor* newspapers. They were laughing as the man was led away. Del found herself wanting to smack them. The speaker system was crackling "Testing, Testing, Testing" and guitar chords were fading in and out. Suzanne went looking for Ray telling Del to stay put. Del had no problem with that since a crush such as this meant there were already too many people in too small a space. She saw some mounted police over by a water fountain. She thought this a horrible place to bring a horse. Definitely there were too many people and more were joining to the rear. At least all types were here: Women Strike For Peace, Quakers looking respectable and reserved, Socialist Workers and Progressive Labor Party functionaries handing out flyers that were now either stuffed into pockets or fluttering to the ground. She saw Tim's friend, Casey, a guitar strapped to his back weaving through the crowd to the staging. A young woman was selling War Resisters League pins and posters.

Suddenly, hearing her name, Dell turned. Jonathan, breathless, stood in front of her. His cheeks were apple red and he was shivering in his brown sweater. He wanted to know where Ray, Tim and Gus were. She pointed over in the direction of the staging and he was off again cutting through the crowd. Someone else jostled her as people pushed forward. Demonstrations become one organism and she didn't like being in the middle of this one but needed to stay put or Suzanne would never find her.

The counter-demonstrators' chants were getting louder now so their numbers must also be increasing. *Drop Dead, Red. Drop Dead, Red. Give Us Joy, Bomb Hanoi*. That last was a new one, she thought. *Burn Yourselves, Not Your Card*. That was repulsive.

When Suzanne reappeared her eyes were bright, their redness replaced with a darting, alert energy.

"Ray is fine," she said. "He seems relaxed. There are tons of press over by the staging. The publicity is going to be great."

Del asked about Tim, and Suzanne reported that he was dressed like wild colonial boy meets barrister. "He's wearing his Irish fisherman's sweater and that beautiful, three-piece herringbone suit he scored in the clothing room. And, Gus–Suzanne kept going–Oh my God, he could never be drafted. He'd want to be a General. He's ordering everyone around. Even the cops are avoiding him."

"And, Miss Day?" Del asked.

"Sitting in a folding chair under a tree," said Suzanne.

— 43 —

Invocation

The microphones were crackling and wheezing and the counter-demonstrators' chants were being drowned out by other chants: **Hell No, We Won't Go** and **What Do We Want? Peace. When Do We Want It? Now**. It was a crazy montage of competing sounds: the crackling of the speaker system, the fusion of chants and now a song added with *This Little Light of Mine* being sung and Casey's guitar chords raw and his high tenor skirling upwards. Several people in the crowd lifted their cigarette lighters aloft, their tiny licks of flame sputtering in the sunlight. It was beginning.

Suzanne and Del inched forward so they had a clear view of the staging and the podium. Choruses were being added to the simple folk tune so, *This Little Light of Mine* was now shining in Hanoi and Saigon and Washington and New York and finally Union Square where the chorus ended with clapping and hooting and the thumping of feet on pavement and earth. The microphones were readjusted for greater height and the Reverend A.J. Muste stepped forward with a thank you to Casey for that wonderful song and a, "Welcome. Welcome to all of you, brothers and sisters united for peace and against war." And the chanting began again. *War No More. War No More.* And it seemed almost possible at that moment that those words repeated and repeated and repeated with such fervor and persistence could not be ignored. Such was their simple belief, their passion, their young and insistent blood.

Dorothy Day felt the chant throbbing in her own temple and looked up at A.J. who she had known now for over twenty years. He stood ramrod straight and reed thin in front of the bank of microphones. She heard his breath amplified through the speakers and wondered about his heart beating and his lungs expanding and all the years of expelling his spirit into a sea of faces before him. How many speeches in his already long life, how many makeshift podiums, how many arrests had the two of them shared over the years? The energized and expectant crowd had its own momentum by now, fueled by the counter-demonstrators' chants that could be heard in more quiet intervals. She suspected that the anti-war chants gained power partly because those chanting wished to pulverize the opposition into plowshares. She remembered Debs own reflection, perhaps made on this very spot, that even a friendly mob has the smell of the beast about it. A.J. had raised his two hands and was pressing the air before him as if to quell the elements.

The chants diminished, wavered and faded into the air, and A.J., the timbre of his voice at eighty still strong, asked for a moment of reflection. Even the counter-demonstrators ceased their turbulence as if two opposing teams were observing an agreed upon ritual before the contest. How strange, Dorothy thought, this welter of images. A.J. in his level and beautifully non-denominational way invoking the God of all their traditions, the God of mercy and justice, the compassionate God who opens up for us the practice of non-violence. He requested a moment of silence in remembrance of Norman Morrison, the Quaker pacifist who had immolated himself in front of the Pentagon just last week.

Then A.J. asked for God's blessing on the young men here today. He asked that we support them and join with them in whatever non-violent way we could–for if there were enough draft card burners, enough young men, indeed, enough of us all willing to say no to war then it would not be possible for society to wage war and what a glorious day that would be, what a glorious day that would be for all sides in this war and what a glorious day that would be for all mankind.

Dorothy had bowed her head for this meditation but raised it as she heard the cadence of language reaching its apex. She caught A.J.'s eyes scanning the crowd and a chill ran through her.

Del usually did not care for preliminary speeches, especially when it was an act of civil disobedience that everyone was there to witness or to participate in, but A.J.'s words lingered and set a somber and respectful tone that she found steadying. She was having a hard time shaking a feeling of being stalked ever since stepping through the barricades with Suzanne. It was an unnerving sensation and wasn't helped by being hemmed in by tall buildings. She had not bowed her head but was instead staring into the crowd in front of her and, in doing so, found herself looking directly at the back of Jonathan Le Blanc's head. He was about fifteen feet in front of her and she didn't know why she was not aware of him before. Caught off-guard, she immediately looked away spooked by an image of cross hairs. The mood was broken by Suzanne squeezing her arm. A.J. was now introducing Brad Nelson, Chairman of the Committee For Non-Violence. Dorothy would be the next to speak.

— 44 —

Speeches

Dorothy liked Brad Nelson although she thought he did have a bit of the patrician about him. He had been jailed many times over the years and was a consciousness objector during the Second World War. The Committee for Non-Violence had been his brainchild, born out of 60 days in solitary at Lewisburg Federal Penitentiary in 1944. Dorothy had read his book about that experience and it remained one of the prison reflection books that most stirred her. Because he was in his twenties during that time, the book reminded her of her own humiliations around that age when she was arrested for the first time in Washington, D.C. in 1917 during a Suffrage demonstration. She had participated in a hunger strike and, because it was her first arrest and imprisonment, it was seared in her memory. At least she had been with others, but Brad had spent 60 days alone and with nothing to read, nothing to divert his attention from the cold and dark. She, on the other hand, after requesting it for three days was given a Bible to read and was able to have conversations with her friend, Polly, through a ventilation vent. The hunger strike lasted only ten days before their demands were met for release but still the sound through that same ventilation system of one of the older, frailer women gagging as she was forced fed was a memory that would not vanish.

Brad, since A.J. was so tall, was busily adjusting the microphone so that it more matched his height. It gave out a squeal amplified by the speakers and the counter-demonstrators began again raising their voices. *GIVE US JOY, BOMB HANOI. GIVE US JOY, BOMB HAN*...Brad's voice, usually a study in modulation and control, broke into their chant with an impassioned, "As someone who has recently returned from Hanoi, I can tell you. Bombs do not give joy nor will they win this war. What will win this war," Brad continued, "is ending this war!" The rally supporters cheered as Brad's voice continued to gain strength and Dorothy thought this might be a longer speech than he was ordinarily inclined to deliver. The chants from across the street had muted although she could still hear them between Brad's pauses. She thought he looked youthful even now into his forties. He cared not a whit for fashion and still wore the classic outfits of his Yale college days cutting an elegant figure in a camel's hair long coat and scarf. Dorothy, herself, was feeling dowdy. She wished she had worn something other than the bulky and mannish coat that Miss Bean had brought her from England. Miss Bean, Dorothy was certain, felt fashion to be one of the devil's workshops and considered it her apostolic duty to insure that bodies be camouflaged in stout wool.

Dorothy in her youth was partial to comfortable but stylish clothes and had no problem showing off the finer features of her form. She had a lovely, long neck with a beautiful clavicle that Graham would stroke with his index finger before placing kisses there and fine high cheekbones and a gamine quality about her eyes. She liked her figure then and enjoyed the fall of a skirt over her hips and the tug of a soft blouse over her breasts. She also loved the Staten Island days when clothes were minimal and she went barefoot wearing Graham's old felt hat supple as chamois in her hands. When he left, she had often crushed that hat to her breasts at night and sobbed into its softness. Memories of that past still intruded upon her even in moments such as these–as if an alternate life still existed that she could step back into.

But Brad was gesturing now in a manner that signaled the end of his remarks. She heard her name being mentioned and Miss Bean beside her was clapping her woolen gloved hands enthusiastically and beaming in her direction and asking if Dorothy wished to have her valise held. Which, of course, she did. And why, for God's sake, had she brought the thing? Augustus appeared at her elbow to assist her up the five or six steps necessary to mount to the podium although she felt perfectly able to ascend herself. Had she been in her twenties such a gesture would have been considered a courtly, gentlemanly flourish; now, at sixty-seven, it had more a feel of the truss about it. Still, she accepted his arm and noticed that he looked quite smart and professorial in a tweed jacket with leather elbow patches. His blue eyes had a sparkle to them that she saw mirrored in the others she knew who were also planning to burn their cards. They were all standing on the right of the platform. Dorothy thanking Gus for his assistance looked over to A.J. and Brad who were on the left. Walking over she gave each a hug which A.J. accepted easily and Brad more formerly. Turning back to the microphone she saw that the height was fine and, touching its cold stem, began to address the chant of, *MOSCOW MARY. MOSCOW MARY*. She quipped how her fame preceded her. But that chant brought with it a whir of memory, a thud on her shoulder, the clatter of horses' hooves, the froth of spittle, the smell of the beast. Another time, another protest in this same place only twenty years past. Dorothy held tightly to the microphone's cold metal and the whir vanished and before her eyes another sea of faces emerged pulling into focus the words that must be said.

"It is our duty to protest this war. It is our duty in whatever way we can to support what these young men will do today. They do it for us all."

Moscow Mary, *Moscow Mary*, kept beat, almost drowning out Dorothy's simple and spare request.

Del had never heard her deliver a speech in such a charged atmosphere. Certainly she had heard Dorothy give talks at Saint Jude's during their regular Friday night meetings. But those were intimate gatherings of mostly like-minded followers. She found herself turning in the direction of the chanters as if facing them could neutralize their voices. Dorothy was talking about the Vietnamese people now, the innocents on all sides caught in the crossfire, the monks burning themselves in Saigon, the litany of so much suffering. She was reminding everyone of Christ's admonition to Peter to put up his sword. And then with her voice rising above the persistent chanters, she introduced the young men who were going to burn their draft cards. Each came forward as his name was called and stood shoulder to shoulder to her right. Dorothy concluded her remarks by acknowledging their enlistment today in that great non-violent army, the only one worth joining if one truly wanted to fight for the continuance of the human race.

With that last line Dorothy released her grip on the microphone watching it wobble slightly as the crowd before her cheered and applauded. Gus came forward and after thanking her publicly for her remarks offered his arm again and led her down the steps, back to Miss Bean, before turning and taking the same steps back up two at a time to the platform where he stood next to Ray. Tim acknowledged Dorothy's words, also, praising her example over the years. Starting with him, each man would issue a brief, personal statement prior to their collective act of civil disobedience. The crowd cheered. Journalists and photographers jockeyed for position. Del looked over at Suzanne. She was looking down at her feet, her left hand clenched into a fist.

Do It

From the angle where Jonathan stood he could see Ray moistening his lips nervously and loosening the knot on his tie. For some reason those actions reminded Jonathan of George Orwell's story in which a condemned prisoner walking to his execution jumps from habit over a puddle. Why bother, considering his fate? How Jonathan hated that image. He had slammed the book shut when he read it. For Jonathan, that jump was the big story, bigger than the noose around the man's neck, the spring of the trap, the snap of the rope. For Jonathan, all the tension and the ache was in that hop over a puddle. For God's sake, just burn the damn thing. Forget the speeches. Burn it now and get it over with.

The five of them had drawn straws for the order of speeches and Ray had drawn the last. He now stood alone in front of the podium. He acknowledged the four who came before him and the eloquence of their individual statements. Then, he squared his shoulders and stated simply that it was every Christian's duty to protest injustice and that sometimes it was the very law itself that was unjust. He referenced the recent law making it a crime to burn a draft card. He stated the irony that made it moral to torch a Vietnamese hut with a Zippo lighter but not to put that flame to a piece of paper. He concluded his remarks with the words that he freely and gladly would burn his draft card today and that no government had the right to make him a hired killer. He said these final words with great force and deliberation. The amplifiers carried every syllable out over the crowd and Suzanne felt a great rush of love for her young husband who had so paced and fretted the night before about his statement and who now threw those words defiantly into the wind.

Del clapped long and hard as did everyone else who realized that the moment was at hand that could well send all of these young men to jail for five years. Both Suzanne and Del were on tiptoes straining to hear every word, to see each movement. A.J. and Brad had come forward as Tim, Ray, Gus, Cliff and Billy formed a semi-circle behind the microphones. Each had taken out his draft card and was holding it up to the crowd. Everyone was quiet, even the counter-demonstrators. Dorothy Day standing in the very front thought how like a concelebrated Mass it seemed. *Hoc est enim corpus Meum.* For this is My body. How true she thought.

Cameras flashed and television crews crowded forward catching footage of every detail. The FBI agents, conspicuous as ever, were taking their own photos. Voices were recorded, notes were taken. Brad lit a wooden match and handed it to Gus who lit his card first and then Tim, Ray, Billy and Cliff immediately touched their cards to that flame. The combined flames surged.

Then it was a squiggle of something in the air. A combined jerk back, a clatter. Then it was, "Watch out." "Get him." People falling backwards into the crowd. Another scrambling clatter of microphones. Another sweeping arc of something in the air. Suzanne and Del were shoved forward pushed by people behind trying to get a better view. "What's happening?" Suzanne yelling, "Do you see Ray?" Del didn't. There was a jumble of blue all around the platform and then the microphones righted and Brad Nelson's voice:

"Please, everyone. Quiet. All is fine. All under control. A minor interruption." Del could now see Ray and Gus laughing and Tim whisking off his vest and suit lapels. Someone threw Cliff a cigarette lighter and he was waving his draft card in the air, calling out to the crowd, "Does anyone have a clothesline?" The culprit with the fire-extinguisher was escorted away by the police. The counter-demonstrators, more confused than anyone, had resumed **Give Us Joy, Bomb Hanoi.** A.J. was talking to Billy while Brad returned to the microphone.

"Well, I must admit, the fire-extinguisher was a nice bit of creative non-violence. But, our spirits have not been dampened even though the draft cards were. We're taking care of that now." The cigarette lighter tossed to Cliff had the loft of a butane torch. They took turns waving their cards above the flame, drying them out. Before an incendiary point was reached, each withdrew his card and then collectively with film rolling and cameras flashing, the draft cards were lit again and officially, individually, collectively and thoroughly went up in flames. Everyone cheered. The counter-demon-strators booed. There was one more chorus of *This Little Light of Mine* and it was over. Life could return to normal.

— 46 —

After

Following the rally, everyone dispersed either going home
in groups, as was advised, or solo. For a large demonstration, it had actually been quite peaceful except for
the Laurel and Hardy incident with the fire-extinguisher.
Only two people had to be escorted away, and they were
counter-demonstrators. Still, Dorothy noticed across
the street as she was heading for the subway with Miss
Bean, a large, red gasoline can prominently displayed
on a third floor fire-escape landing. She shuddered,
remembering the Quaker who had immolated himself
just days before at the Pentagon in front of Defense
Secretary Robert McNamara's window. The act A.J.
had referred to in his Invocation as containing, *An element of history, an element of terror, an element of
courage and an element of mystery.* What could be
said beyond that, she thought. Still that silent warn-
ing or desire or portent planted conspicuously on the
fire escape landing rattled her. She found herself more

troubled by the afternoon's events than she had antic- ipated and upon returning to Saint Jude's retired to her room. Miss Bean, feeling invigorated by the out- ing, said she would later bring up a square of the ritual Saturday Shepherd's Pie that she was making for the evening meal.

Leaving the rally site, Jonathan walked up to Belle- vue Hospital where he stayed sitting beside Mercedes' bed for half an hour before leaving in a state of agi- tation. She was almost completely unresponsive. He held her hand and squeezed it but she gave no return- ing pressure. Her hand was hot and limp. Her sleep seemed drugged and her eye movements behind closed lids darted here and there as if she were watching some frenetic, plot-less movie. He told her about the demon- stration and then felt stupid since nothing in her aspect registered awareness. He tried to calm himself by say- ing he knew her mother was here. The doctors might be trying new medications. He lifted the chart at the end of the bed and saw some different notations where the medications were listed, then placed the chart back. Taking a deep breath, he leaned over the side of the bed and quickly kissed her forehead. His lips felt scorched. He wanted to scream but whispered, "I'll be back to see you tomorrow. I love you." Then, he left.

Gus, Tim and Ray met up again with Billy and Cliff at Lafayette Street where they all went back to debrief. Brad was there as well as an ACLU lawyer who was interested in taking their case were they to be charged collectively with breaking the new law. The lawyer had done work in the past for some of the other anti-war groups based at Lafayette and wanted to offer his services. Gus was suspicious and said he didn't want any ambulance chasers sniffing around even if they were ACLU types. Tim thought the lawyer was an ok guy and said there was no harm in hearing him out. The meeting was short since there really was nothing to do but wait until the Justice Department made its move. The lawyer gave a brief presentation along with his card and left. Brad, noticing Gus's irritation with each repeated pull on his pipe, volunteered that one thing he had learned after more than one jailing was that it made good sense to know all your options even the ones you were convinced you opposed. Like a chess game, every strategy should be known and at your fingertips. This quieted Gus who had immense respect for Brad. They discussed the pros and cons of the rally and then worked up a brief collective statement to be issued pending a move by Justice.

Suzanne and Del walked east on Fourteenth, past Kline's. The paddy wagons were gone. Now, it was just another Saturday with shoppers, cooking smells, hawkers barking their wares. Del saw Frankie the Pretzel Man making his rounds. She suggested getting a cab but Suzanne said she needed to walk so they decided to continue on to Second Avenue, then take the bus down to Houston and walk to the apartment from there. Ray had told Suzanne he had to go to Lafayette after the demonstration even though she had wanted him to come right home. She was upset by this, Del knew, but she didn't want to be caught in the middle of their disagreements. Suzanne was saying something about Christmas, about how this day was like having all the presents unwrapped and the colored paper littering the floor, about the empty feeling after, you know? Del agreed, mumbling, "I know." Suddenly, Suzanne stopped and said, "No, you don't know, Del. You weren't even listening."

Suzanne's jaw was clenched, her face flushed. Del reached out to touch her arm and was pushed away. "You know," said Suzanne, "I just won't be able to stand it if you don't listen to me too. Two weeks of Ray waking up in the middle of the night, going into the kitchen, looking irritated at me if I came out to be with him. Basically, just tolerating me. I can't stand it and now, who knows what's next?" Del apologized. They were facing each other in the blur of Fourteenth Street. People walking by them, looking, wondering. Some guy passing saying, "Hey, Lezzies." Suzanne continuing, "You have got to listen to me, Del. I can't live with that brooding man if I can't talk to someone."

They did not catch the bus that afternoon, but walked down to the Second Avenue Deli and sat at a window booth and ordered matzoh ball soup and talked for a long time about everything that had happened that day and about what might happen in the future.

Waiting

The news coverage was beyond expectation. On Saturday night, the major television networks gave ample time to the speakers and the draft card burning complete with the fire-extinguisher incident. It was well filmed and strangely riveting to watch the cards curling up in flame as the crowd sang, *This Little Light of Mine.* Next morning, **The Sunday New York Times** carried a prominent feature story on the third page with a photograph of all five looking sober as preachers in their suits and staring intently at the flaming cards. "Perfect," said Tim.

It was early morning and they were all at the House drinking Ed's coffee with the **Times** spread out on one of the tables. It was no secret that the apartments and the House were under surveillance. Del thought it a ridiculous choreography, the whole G-man, Dick Tracy element, until she remembered Dewey being hijacked on the Bowery only months before. There was a car now permanently parked across the street from the apartments in front of the Italian Social Club as well as one down from the House. Men wearing hats sat inside each car reading the paper or drinking coffee. They didn't even make a pretense of disguise. "Nope," said Tim. "Just waiting on paperwork."

That Sunday afternoon, they all joined the thousands marching down Fifth Avenue in what was to date the largest END THE WAR NOW march in the City of New York.

On Monday, Tim and Ray got out the old Chevy to take a run down to the Fulton Fish Market to pick up some crates of mangoes that Delucca called to say he was saving for them. As soon as they pulled out into the street, the black sedan over by the park swung immediately behind them. Ray turned around and said, "Christ, the Hats are coming too. I don't believe it. Don't they have any real crooks to catch?"

Tim checked out the rear view mirror. "They must be bored. Let's have some fun."

For the next few miles, Tim did a hop-scotch route around the city, making a right on Canal and then an immediate left onto Elizabeth with a quick right onto Bayard and then a left onto Center. Ray, frowning and peering out the side-view mirror, cautioned him to be cool. Not to make any mistakes. "We don't want to get busted on any cheap traffic charge."

Tim was grinning. "I'm obeying all the rules. Using my signals. Are their hats still on?"

Ray, nervous but beginning to enjoy himself, reported back that all hats were firmly in place. "They're like robots."

Tim stayed on Center and then slowed down to make three very slow, very intentional and very sleep-inducing circles around Foley Square, the dutiful black car following right behind. Ray shook his head, "Like robots."

After the pas de deux around Foley Square, Tim took a straight run to Fulton. Both he and Ray got out and parking across from Delucca's stall, loaded up three crates of perfectly ripe, on-the-cusp-of-going-rotten mangoes. Delucca was his usual voluble self going on about life and how he saw youze guys on the tube. "Nice suit," he nodded at Tim. "You, too, Ray, but your tie looked tight."

"Hey, ya know? It's your business. You do what ya gotta do. My old man, he hated Mussolini and he hated uniforms. Everybody's got a beef."

Tim rubbed some mango juice from his hands onto his jeans. "Yup, everybody's got a beef. Just like those guys." He jerked his thumb in the direction of the sedan parked two stalls down and across the street.

"No kiddin'," said Delucca. "On your tail?"

Tim pulled out a cigar and started peeling off the cellophane. "All the way from Chrystie." He was chuckling and lighting up.

Delucca laughed. "Marron. It's stupid. Youze guys are all right."

"Hey." Delucca went over to a shelf behind the stall. "Give these knockers to the Ginny for me." He produced two beautifully fragrant, ripe melons. Tim winked.

"Will do."

Delucca stared disgustedly at the snoop-car and then after slamming Tim's door stood back and waved goodbye as both cars slowly drove down Fulton.

To keep up the game, Tim took the long way back to Saint Jude's. As they were unloading the mangoes in front of the House, the black sedan resumed its old position. After the last crate was put in the pantry, Ray leaned against the hood of the Chevy waiting for Tim to return from delivering the "knockers" to Italian Mike. When Tim came back, they both leaned against the car and looked down the street at their followers. Ray was scowling. "Junkies and dealers doing their thing night and day in that park and that's all those guys over there can do? So fuckin' stupid."

— 48 —

Birthday

Sometimes Dorothy Day wondered if she had squandered her life. People called her a saint, she knew, but she dismissed the idea. They wanted to see her life as extraordinary, heroic, but doing that was too easy. It made it look as if living such a life were impossible to do and, anyway, maybe what others saw as self-sacrifice could also be avoidance. Maybe she should have struggled harder to stay with Graham those many years ago. Maybe becoming baptized was the final way to push him out. Maybe she had not told him enough how much she loved him and that converting to Catholicism did not mean she loved him less. Maybe. Maybe. She had stubbornly set her course and had not altered it. So, he left and she raised Cara herself within the Catholic Worker community which meant she was often an absent mother letting her daughter be cared for by others while she wrote and worried about Saint Jude's finances and increasingly went on pilgrimage. She knew

living in community meant that a child had many mothers and fathers, but it also meant, and this she felt as
a deep wound in her heart, it also meant neglect and it
pained her, just as a life without Graham's lean body
next to her, waking with his head on her breast, just as
that absence still pained her and she had a hard time,
a hard time, even now entering into her sixty-eighth
year with those thoughts.

That evening she had asked Timothy Barnes to
come visit her. She wanted to talk about Saturday's
demonstration but upon seeing him she surprised herself by asking a totally different question. She knew
that he and Del were seeing one another and so she
asked how they were doing. She liked the girl but there
was something about her, some planting of feet too
deeply into the ground, that Dorothy recognized and
it concerned her. Tim was evasive. So she asked if he
had proposed marriage and he laughed.

"Dorothy, I'm not in much of a position to propose
marriage to anyone. I'm two stones shy of a jail bird if
that's even an expression." He said this and then said
he didn't think Del was in love with him, that she was,
perhaps, more interested in Jonathan, or, and then he
laughed in a funny way, or, in no one. He said he'd
love to marry her and have a little apartment like Ray
and Suzanne but that seemed as far away as the man
in the moon.

Dorothy startled herself, then, by saying that she
thought he should ask her. That way he would know

and Del would have a chance to say yes or no.

He had seemed quite taken aback and said that he couldn't talk about this now and besides too much was happening. But, Dorothy persisted, too much was always happening.

She looked at Timothy Barnes and she didn't see Graham but she did see a young man who was giving up on a young woman who Dorothy suspected was not given to bending. She reached out to him then and covered his hand with her own as it rested on his knee. It still looked like an adolescent's hand with chewed fingernails. Tears came to her eyes.

Timothy rose from his chair, confused she was sure, and asked if she were all right? Asked if he had upset her? She said, "No." But, she did thank him for coming over and asked him to talk to Del. Just a few words.

What was that all about, she thought, after he left. It was her birthday today. Perhaps that's what had stirred her up.

That Night

Tim also wondered what that was about. Dorothy had never spoken to him concerning such private matters. There were the occasional, oblique inquiries about his nocturnal habits. But those were usually sidebars to other conversations and could be deflected by a rakish puff of cigar smoke or an innocent shrug of shoulder. This was a sit down, direct conversation about his personal life and affections. Maybe it was an after-effect of the draft card burning. It hit people differently when they knew you were waiting for the other shoe to drop.

On the way back to the apartment, Tim stopped at the corner bodega on Kenmare and Mott and bought a quart of milk, a can of corned beef hash and a dozen eggs. Stepping outside, he noticed that the light was on in the women's apartment. Should he? There was a faint drizzle of rain coming down, more of a cold, damp mist in the November dark. The omnipresent sedan was parked at its usual station by the Italian

Social Club. Maybe Del would like some eggs and hash. What the hell.

Without giving it much thought, he crossed the street, bounded up the stairs and rapped on the door. Del answered on the third knock. She looked hesitant but not unhappy to see him. She said Jonathan had just been there and had left moments before to visit Mercedes. She thought the knock might be him returning, trying to get her to go up one more time. "He's so intense." is what she said. Tim said he bought eggs and hash and would she like to join him for a quick meal and she said yes. He said great and that was that.

Of course, after hearing Tim going up the stairs, Del had second thoughts. But, she craved normalcy that night. She missed Tim's easy banter. What was annoying could also be comforting. Sitting in the men's apartment, cooking up eggs and hash. Getting out ketchup, perking the coffee in the beat-up aluminum pot. She craved it all. She wanted to sit in front of the mouth of the open oven and be tended to. Also, Tim was so simple and forthcoming. She, on the other hand, always seemed to be holding something back or protecting someone. When asked to say who or what was pre-occupying her, Del would get a distant look, deflect the question, say it was nothing or that she didn't know. But that night, she knew sitting with Tim in a warm kitchen was all the intensity she wanted.

Tim measured grounds into the percolator basket, filled the bottom half with water and put the whole thing on the flame. Using a dishtowel, he wiped the iron skillet. Then, adding a chunk of margarine, he put the skillet back down on the front burner. He grabbed the can of hash, the miserable can-opener working for once in its life, and opening up the can scooped two mounds of hash onto the middle of the skillet. They sizzled.

A few minutes later, Del was sitting on the red, cracked vinyl chair next to the stove. She hadn't kissed him when she entered, but mussed his hair and said the coffee smelled good. Tim made two dents in the mounds of hash and plopped an egg into each. The scene was cozy and domestic and for one extravagant moment he considered flinging himself on his knees and begging for her hand in marriage. The next second, he was chuckling at the absurdity and she said, "What's so funny?"

"Nothing," he said. "I just had a crazy, far-out thought. Want some grub?"

She nodded. "It smells wonderful."He poured two cups of coffee into mugs and dished up the plates. He pulled a half-loaf of Wonder Bread from the top of the refrigerator and, un-twirling the cellophane bag, spilled out four slices and tossed them onto the plates. She got out ketchup and the quart of milk and put them on the table. They both sat down, ready to dig in, when someone knocked at the door.

— 50 —

A Simple Question

Del heard Jonathan's voice. Tim asked him if he wanted to come in, but Jonathan said no. Then he asked if Del were there and, if so, he needed to talk with her. Del did not want to talk to Jonathan Le Blanc that night. She wanted to stay right where she was and eat eggs and hash. She looked up and could see Jonathan's right shoulder over Tim's left and wanted to hide, disappear, but Tim turned sideways and with a shrug let Jonathan's question fall into the room. Del put down her fork and Jonathan said, "It'll only take a minute. I need to ask you something."

She followed him down the stairs. He was walking quickly. She had to hurry to catch up. He went out the first set of doors, crossed the small tiled entry way, pushed open the heavy exterior doors and stood on the sidewalk looking up as she came outside. His face was flushed and his eyes looked unnaturally bright. He was wearing his usual brown sweater with the sleeves pushed up. His hair, curling in the light rain, seemed to shimmer. A street light behind him gave off a strange backlit pulsation. "What's wrong?" she asked. He looked at her with a mix of agitation, desperation and something else she could not identify.

"She's dying," he said. "I can see it and they can't do a thing about it and they still don't know what's causing it. Not only can't she walk, but she has absolutely no sensation in either her arms or legs. None at all. I could squeeze her leg with all my might and she wouldn't feel a thing. It's just moving up her body. This thing. They're talking about hooking her up to a ventilator. They were saying all this right in front of her and she's looking at me and shaking her head from side to side– I don't know anymore what she wants." He stopped abruptly and stood like a man at attention. Like he was alert and waiting for something. Some word or sign. The wind picked up and Del could see a veil of mist pass in front of the street lamp. She was feeling the same creepy cross-hair sensation that she had felt at the demonstration on Saturday. She tried to shake it off.

"Let's step inside, Jonathan. I'm freezing." She pushed open the exterior door with her back and they both stood inside the little foyer sandwiched between the two sets of doors and lit by one dim light bulb screwed into a lintel socket. Jonathan's agitation came with him into the little space but after his outside outburst, he seemed calmer.

He stood in the opposite corner still positioned as if at attention, the same unnatural light in his eyes.

"Ok. Ok." he said. "Listen. Do you think people can take one another's pain?"

He asked this with clipped urgency as if any response should be definitive and uncontested. Perhaps it was the smallness of the space, the dimness of the light, the mist moving outside, but Del felt she needed to back up, to put him farther from her.

"You mean like Mercedes, Jonathan? Her pain. Is that what you're talking about?" *Let's be reasonable here* is what Del was thinking. Let's have a reasonable discussion, one that doesn't pulse like the light outside or the bulb above that gutters like a candle.

"Mercedes, yes. Her pain. And others, too, like Tim and Ray and Gus. There's that car outside. All of it. All the crazy, uncertain pain."

Del needed to get a grip on this conversation. "I have no idea, Jonathan. Really, no idea. It's too much. I can't talk about this now. I really can't. I'm used up."

As soon as those words were out, Del knew they were right. Craven but right. She was used up and didn't want to talk with him any more. She had nothing more to say. There was no reason for her to be standing there. Jonathan's face had a quizzical look, the kind of cryptic half-smile, half-purse to his lips he would sometimes get before he said something or took off.

"Yeah. You're right. It is too much. All of it."

She had her hand on the doorknob behind her and was turning it, saying, "I've got to go."

"One more question. Just one. You do believe there is a God, don't you?"

Her hand stalled and she looked at him. She wanted to laugh, then stopped, stunned. How could the answer to this one, elemental question, this question that should be the easiest one for her to answer given the work they all were doing suddenly be a complete unknown?

"I don't know," she said.

Part of her was saying to herself. Just say *yes* and get out of here. Just tell him you believe, of course you do. But she found herself matching his stare and, for a moment, feeling calm.

"I don't know, Jonathan. I don't know about believing in God. But, I do know there is something. Some energy out there that I can't explain. I feel it."

"Yeah. Yeah." He said this softly, almost to himself. "It's something, isn't it? Hard to explain."

"I'm going upstairs now."

Del stood there wondering if he'd object, but he was just looking at her and leaning back into the exterior door. He thanked her for talking with him and smiled. He said, "It helped."

She waved goodnight and hurried up the four flights of stairs. When she opened the apartment door, Tim was sitting there reading the paper, his stocking feet resting on the open oven door.

Night Thoughts

Dorothy Day had felt on edge all day. The conversation with Timothy had only added to her sense of the lateness of time and things undone. Oft times on her birthday she would get this feeling of trepidation. How had yet another year managed to come about and pass? And now, sixty-eight? Amazing. In her twenties she never gave mortality a thought unless to assume she might not live a long life. Now in her late sixties death seemed to reside in an ante-chamber, quite content to rest there in the shadow of her thoughts. She preferred the attitude of her twenties. This "chamber" business was morbid. Maybe she needed a trip. The autumn darkness seemed to come earlier this year. The cold, too, or maybe it was age.

She remembered when she and Graham lived out on Staten Island, how they would run about on the beach in December collecting driftwood, dressed only in cotton pants and old sweaters. They were happy and hearty and never had a sniffle. She was lucky to get through a winter now without at least one bout of flu. She had an invitation to visit Christ In The Desert Monastery in New Mexico this year and was thinking it would be beneficial to do so in January and then she could continue on west and visit the Catholic Worker communities in California. She could visit César in Delano. It would be good to see him and his family again. She knew the timing of her pilgrimages was often the brunt of jokes around Saint Jude's and she did feel some guilt about abandoning everyone to the city winter. She promised herself she would stay here through Christmas.

She riffled through correspondence on her desk and then picked up her daily Missal, placing the ribbon marker on tomorrow's date, November 9, Saint Theodore, Martyr. She read the brief annotation under the date: *Martyred in Asia Minor. In the act of being martyred, he continually offered up prayers and praise to God in thanksgiving.* How did they know about Saint Theodore's demeanor, she wondered. What proof had they? Why must we meditate on the horrific act of martyrdom coupled with prayers and praise? Wasn't it enough that blood was shed for one's faith? Graham would say that it was religious, sadomasochistic, sexual sublimation, this insistence on exalting God while the executioner's ax was poised. Truth was, she too felt uneasy about idealizing martyrdom. She had seen too much common, unsung, martyrdom in county hospitals, tenements and jails to be enraptured with this more ostentatious form. She didn't know if this counted as a minor heresy but there it was. It was not a sin she would confess. She remembered when she was a new convert. The sins she would confess!

She thought of the old priest on Staten Island who was her first Confessor. She had gone to confession every week then. He was so deaf, penitents had to shout their sins into the man's ear. She had even seen people leave the church during confessional hours when they discovered he was the confessor. But, she was ardent. She once accused herself of the boastful sin of "vainglory" and the old priest laughed. "How did you do that, my child?" When she confessed she had pridefully challenged Sister Camillia, her catechism instructor, on her interpretation of *the near occasions of sin,* the old priest laughed again and said that a few "near occasions" would do Sister Camillia a world of good and cautioned Dorothy not to worry about pride or vainglory and gave her the usual five Our Fathers and five Hail Marys and to say a little prayer for him, please, to the Blessed Mother. The scruples of the newly converted.

She smiled at the recollection and fingered the prayer card that lay beside her Missal. There, written on the card, were the names of all those she prayed for over the years, the old priest and Graham included.

She placed the card inside her Missal. Tomorrow would dawn. New prayers and new occasions for prayer would reveal themselves. Of this, she was certain.

— 52 —

Taken By Surprise

After talking with Del, Jonathan walked over to the park across from Saint Jude's, sat down on a bench and smoked a cigarette. The light rain was still falling and he felt it steaming off his body. He had felt warm ever since leaving Mercedes and wondered if he were getting sick. But, he felt fine, alert, happy even. He felt as if he had all the time and all the energy to do anything he chose. The big storefront window in Saint Jude's was still lit up. Smokey was sitting at the desk. Jonathan could see his profile in the lighted window, a chin worthy of Mount Rushmore. He heard talking as the door to Saint Jude's opened and three figures left. New volunteers for the evening meal maybe. He didn't recognize the voices. Everyone came and everyone left and, in between, lives were changed. He smiled at the progression. A calmness was settling upon him, taking him quite by surprise. He had felt something beginning to shift while talking with Del. She looked frightened.

179

She needn't have. But, he felt she must have sensed some change too because of that last question, the one where he asked about God and she looked as though she were going to laugh or cry. An alarm came into her eyes and then it left. Maybe she was mirroring the fright going out of his own body. And, then, they had agreed, not on the word God, but on the feeling, the knowledge of something unseen that was present and uncontested and worthy of belief. It was a comfort that two people could agree on the existence of the unseen in these foreboding times.

He took another deep drag of cigarette and lifted his head to look at the moving mist before the street lamp. The mist fell like a golden curtain, a tabernacle veil. The street lamp's shimmering corona made a fitting host. These images often came to him. He thought he was always being bushwhacked by God.

The storefront light went out and he heard Smokey and Ed leaving, Ed calling out "Goodnight" to Gus and the door closing. The city seemed unnaturally quiet tonight. Like it was holding its breath. Odd because he felt so alert, so awake and wasn't quite sure what to do with all the energy. He thought he should use it, do something that would gather it all up into a huge ball and send it rolling down a hill. What would happen then? This force careening down a hill? He stood up and took a final drag, threw down his cigarette and ground it out with the toe of his sneaker. He looked at the spot, nothing left. The ash had become sidewalk, the bits of white paper already melting in the light rain. Everything became something else after awhile. Transformed. Maybe that was the thing about pain too. Maybe pain could be transformed into something else. Rewired so it ran through different circuitry, took a different path. Something spontaneous and abrupt– then change and transformation.

He thought about the time he saved his brother. How totally shocked he was when he did that, running out onto the thin ice, flopping down and feeling it give under him but hold. It felt like a soft net and how he had reached and grabbed his brother's hair in both hands tugging him to shore. How his body felt on fire, his arms like pistons, his sweat seeming to scald the ice into slush. He felt he could do something like that again tonight.

53

Three Windows

Mercedes thought a terrible world surrounded her. This world of smells and sounds, her own and others, and no way to say yes or no. Her neck felt tight, a hinge needing oil. She was the Tin Woodsman in *The Wizard of Oz*, all spare parts and rusting. She heard her heart beating like a great drum in her ears. An unrelenting throb, the thud of blood against thin membrane. Africa.

Jonathan had been here tonight, she knew, but she was unable to make contact. The doctors talked as if she were a stone. But she heard every word. Progressive paralysis. Loss of exterior sensation. Ataxia. Hair samples. Blood work. Ventilator. She could see anger flash in Jonathan's eyes and, of course, that would not work. She didn't suppose she had helped the situation with her embarrassing twitches and grunts. He hadn't stayed long but she wished he had. She didn't need him to solve or do anything. She just wanted him near.

*

Ray had another meeting at Lafayette Street since the FBI had been questioning his parents again in New Jersey. He decided to talk to the ACLU lawyer to see if the re-visitation might signal an imminent arrest. After he returned home, he and Suzanne had a simple supper together and decided to go to bed early. Suzanne had cooked. He had washed the dishes and was now stretched out on the bed in their bedroom.

Suzanne was staring into the bathroom mirror. She was pale and had dark circles under her eyes. They had spoken little while eating, perhaps not wanting to risk an argument. Where, she thought, staring at herself, was the lightheartedness? Where had the feeling gone that they had on the rooftop? She put a warm washcloth to her face and held it there and then felt her eyes begin to sting. I can't start crying now, she said to herself. I can't. I won't.

She shook her head. She brushed her teeth and then picking up her hairbrush ran it quickly through her hair. She was wearing an old pair of pink baby-doll pajamas that seemed ridiculous now, but the waist was well stretched and comfortable. She still had great legs is what she thought looking down and over her stomach. She dabbed some Emerald between her breasts feeling what the hell and left the bathroom.

Hearing her enter the room, Ray opened his eyes and smiled. She came over and sat next to him on the

bed lacing her fingers through the fingers of his out-
stretched hand. They looked at one another until Ray
said, "Life's gotten complicated, hasn't it?" Suzanne
nodded. He sighed and sitting up wrapped both his
arms around his wife. They stayed like that for a long
time.

*

Tim swung his feet off the oven door and seeing
Del's expression wanted to know what Jonathan had
said. She told him about the conversation, leaving
out the last question about God. Tim was shaking
his head saying how Jonathan needed to give himself
a break. He drove himself. He thought too much. He
shouldn't be going up to Bellevue every day. While
Del had to agree with most of that, it annoyed her that
Tim was saying it. They weren't being much help, she
said. Hardly ever visiting her. Then she blurted out
how Jonathan was also worried about him and about
Ray and about Gus. Tim scowled and started to say
something. Then, thinking better of it, he stopped and
asked Del if she wanted to finish her eggs and hash.
He had put the plate in the oven to keep warm. But,
she had lost her appetite. She was sorry for Tim and
also for herself. He had made the effort. Now she felt
preoccupied and just wanted to be alone.

Tim knew when confronted with this kind of skid
that he needed alternatives, so he asked if she wanted to

watch the game on the tube. Del thought for a moment that television might be a good mindless way to salvage the evening but remembering the room, the bed, the TV, it all seemed headed toward complications. She thanked him and said, "No, but thanks."

"How about after the game then?" He was being persistent. "You didn't have anything to eat. We could go get a dog at Weitzman's later. Take a little walk down Delancey."

Sometimes, you just give in, which is what she did. She asked him to come down later, knock and see if she were up.

54

What If

Back in her apartment, the conversation with Jonathan kept replaying in her mind. He was so extreme, so annoyingly intense. She remembered, when he first arrived at Saint Jude's, how they once went out to get a cup of coffee at Jose's Diner. Jonathan got conned into sinking a pocketful of change into the diner payphone for a wino he had invited in to join them for apple pie. The guy insisted on calling his sister in Kansas. Jonathan ended up talking to the sister who gave him an earful and told him to tell her brother to go to hell but first to pay her back the five hundred god-damn dollars she loaned him three years ago, you bastard. Jonathan rephrased the request and after Jose gave him the eye, walked the wino outside making sure he had a cup of coffee to go and a wrapped wedge of pie. She let it happen. She'd done things just as stupid when she first arrived. When he returned, she said something to that effect but Jonathan shot back with, "And, so, did

Christ ever learn?" Then, they were off and running.

Now as she recalled that former, theological debate, she remembered that they ended up agreeing on the fanciful speculation that it would be great if New York City all of a sudden came to a halt. The subways stopped. The escalators stopped. The revolving doors stopped. The elevators stopped. If people unfixed their faces and realized the one another which was God. But this night, Del didn't want speculations. She wanted simplicity.

So, later on when she heard Tim's knock, she jumped off the bed, her clothes still on. She heard Sadie grumbling from behind her door, "Jesus. Jesus, Mary and Joseph. For you, Della Ella. It's late, late. The little Banty. Turn off your light. Go to bed. God dammit."

"Let's get that dog," Tim said. Moments later, they were out the door. Walking down the street, he slipped his hand into hers and she didn't pull away.

Would Jonathan have picked that particular doorway to stand in and have a cigarette had he known Del and Tim would be walking by him that night? Who knows? In the big picture, the way things were shaping up, maybe that was exactly the doorway in which he needed to lean, looking out at the Bowery traffic, surveying the blasted kingdom, smoking the last cigarette in the pack.

Tim saw him first and waved. Del stared.

Jonathan thought she could get a "look." Like his relatives in Canada, something icy and inward and remote in her eyes. But, Tim? He was like an amiable puppy.

"Hey man," Tim said right away. "What's happenin'?" Jonathan shrugged. "We're gonna get a dog. Want one too?"

The truth was he was starved so he said, "Yes, I'd love to" and fell in step. He knew Del wasn't happy about that. She'd had enough of him for one evening. Of this he was sure. Maybe he knew even then what he was going to do. He felt relaxed and conversational, the mist no longer ominous but cool and soothing on his face.

It was true that Del was not keen on Jonathan Le Blanc joining them that night and she didn't hide that sentiment. But, he and Tim did the talking. Weitzman's Deli was way down on Delancey, almost to the Williamsburg Bridge. It was open until one in the morning and famous for making its own "toothsome," as Tim would say, "dogs." They scooted into a booth about midnight. Del slid in first, farthest against the wall. Tim sat next to her and Jonathan opposite him where the two of them continued to talk about all the subjects she preferred not to discuss.

The waiter came and they each ordered a hotdog with sauerkraut and a glass of tea. He scribbled on a pad, put the pencil behind his ear and left. Moments later their food and tea arrived. All Del's attention went to her plate. The bun was soft and white and the sausage itself a plump wonder. The sauerkraut was heaped in the middle so she took care to smooth it out before slathering on the spicy mustard. Then, she bit and from the first snap through the skin, relished every wonderful, sog-filled bite of that hotdog.

Tim and Jonathan were eating and talking, eating and talking. She heard names of Vietnamese villages. She heard body bags. She heard refusal. She heard McNamara and massacre and Zippo lighter. She heard student deferment and draft cards and burning and jail. She heard mention of a single spontaneous act.

Did Del stop then and calibrate anything when she heard those last words? Who said that? Of course, it was him. It was the kind of declaration Jonathan would make. What was he thinking? Or had he already thought it?

They finished their tea. The waiter cleared the dishes. Tim paid the bill, waving Jonathan's offer away.

They said their good nights standing in front of Weitzman's. Jonathan said he was going to stay at Brother Jeffrey's that night. The apartment was close by the East River and he had a key. Brother Jeffrey was out of town for a few days and had asked him to check in on the apartment. Del vaguely wondered if Jonathan were making up the story so he wouldn't have to walk back to the apartments with them. But, she wasn't disappointed. She remembered waving to him and his waving back. She remembered the warmth of Tim's hand in hers and how their shoulders occasionally bumped as they put their heads down and walked home fast, partly because of the lateness of the hour, partly because of the night's damp chill and, for Tim, partly because he was hoping that the swift good night kiss he later received meant more than it did.

55

Waiting

Del locked the door behind her convinced she had made a big mistake going out with Tim. But, she could undo it, set it straight later. She wound the alarm clock on the window ledge next to her bed noting the time was 1:35. She yawned and set the alarm for eight o'clock. Tomorrow or, she corrected herself, today, she was down to cook dinner for the House. It was Tuesday. Tuesday was a meatloaf night. Something comforting in that. Sadie would crow, "Meatloaf. Meatloaf. Della Ella, the Meatloaf Girl. Yeah, Yeah. Meatloaf Girl." Del placed the clock back on the ledge, went into the kitchen to brush her teeth and then, returning, put on her flannel nightgown. She turned down the covers, slipped into bed and clicked off the lamp. Shivering, she waited for her body heat to warm the sheets, alert to the ticking of the clock.

There are mythologies and scientific hypotheses about the deep hours proceeding dawn–the Hour of the Wolf, the hours most people die, the hours most children are born. The hours when regret sits most stubbornly on chests, when worries multiply. For monks and nuns who keep the Liturgy of the Hours, this is the time when the earth is believed to be most vulnerable to attack, so with silent prayer, sacred readings and chant, they keep watch. The shepherds are awake, alert over their flock, the sleeping world spinning. The monks and nuns chant. They know the young lions are crouching and that the snares are set, that the serpents and scorpions lie in wait. They chant. Dawn will come and light and resurrection.

It was still dark when Del felt a fluttering in her ear along with a disturbance of air and then a sense of bright light entering the kitchen. She was frightened. She thought she must be dreaming. Her eyes were closed. What did she mean by disturbance of air? It was like a wind entering and exiting the apartment, restless and urgent. Dreams can be like that, fragments evaporating as soon as they appear, leaving a disquieting sense. Was she dreaming? She didn't think so.

Then minutes, moments later, she did hear someone enter the apartment. Someone parted the curtain that served as her door. Her shoulder was shaken, her name whispered. She listened to words she was, surprisingly, not surprised to hear. "Come next door. There is a man on the phone. You must speak to him. Something has happened. Jonathan has burned himself."

56

Why

Jonathan knew instantly he had made a colossal mistake. Gone too far again. Impetuous. He felt a whoosh of violent wind, was tossed into a dense red-blackness, a uterine seizure. Where was he? He heard questions. He gave answers.

Did this as a religious act.
So no one could stop me.
Against war. All wars.
Give me water. Water.

*

Following Miss Bean out of the room, Del saw two envelopes secured with a rubber band resting on the kitchen floor before the door. Del's name was written on a torn piece of paper tucked under the band. Had Miss Bean not seen them? She picked them up and followed Miss Bean next door. Miss Bean pointed to the phone on her unmade bed, the receiver off.

"I must hurry to the House. You talk to this man."

So, Del heard the events from the *Journal American* reporter. Getting his copy ready for the afternoon edition. Getting some quotes. Getting ready for the headline, **Human Torch**–the story that in twelve hours would be lost.

*

After pushing the envelopes under Del's door, Jonathan walked to an all night gas station on Houston and paid for three gallons of gasoline. The attendant shrugged off a deposit for the can, calling out, "I trust ya." Hefting the can, Jonathan turned and headed to First Avenue walking fast now because the city would soon start to awaken. He walked without looking right or left, pausing only to shift the weight of the can in his hands. When he reached 42nd Street and First Avenue, he crossed to the concrete island in the middle of the intersection and stood facing the darkened shape of the United Nations. He squared his shoulders, took a deep breath and unscrewed the lid of the can. He squeezed his eyes shut pouring the gasoline over the top of his head wetting down his hair and shoulders, torso and pants. He took the gasoline can and carefully placed it on the curb away from where he stood. Then he returned. The sky was beginning to lighten. He stood for a moment and moved his lips. Then, he sat cross-legged on the cold concrete and removed the book of matches tucked into his sock for safety. He pushed open its cover. He pinched free a match.

What the Paper Said

A young pacifist set himself on fire outside the United Nations headquarters in Midtown Manhattan. Apparently going into shock and delirium, he mumbled to attendants and police in the ambulance ride to Bellevue Hospital:

"I am anti-war, all wars. Give me water."

When asked if he did this to protest what was going on in Vietnam, he said, "No.

"I did this as a religious action.

"Water.

"I did this at this hour so nobody could stop me."

A UN Guard standing in the sentry booth near 43rd and First Avenue first saw the flames—"All on fire, rolling and screaming."

Four other UN Guards rushed outside with a hand extinguisher.

The police came. An ambulance from Bellevue pulled up.

The guard helped put him in the ambulance. He kept mumbling, over and over.

"Give me water. Give me water."

On the ambulance ride to Bellevue Hospital he said he was a Catholic Worker.

Left behind at the fire scene were the soles of his charred sneakers, a singed sock, a quarter, a dime, two pennies and a key.

His wallet was charred but the contents were undamaged. It contained two $1 dollar bills, his selective service card, and a snapshot of him and a dark-haired girl.

His watch, still on his wrist, stopped at 5:20 a.m.

Journal American, 11/9/65

— 58 —

Messenger

After talking to the reporter on Miss Bean's phone, Del returned to her apartment, sat on her bed and tore open one of the envelopes. Her hands were shaking. There was something written about Christ, something written about crucifixion and then she saw the word "Mother." She looked at the envelope. It was addressed to his mother. The other letter was addressed to a girl Del knew he liked who lived in New Jersey. So, Del was the messenger. It was hard to catch her breath. She looked at her clock on the window ledge. It said 5:20. Impossible. It was much later than that. She shook it. She wound it. It would not tick. It had stopped. She placed it back on the ledge and hurriedly dressed.

When she got to the House, the place was in an uproar. Miss Day was upstairs answering calls from the media and also conferring with Gus on the draft of a statement for the press. She was horrified, stricken really. She remembered the feeling that she had last night and now this horrible thing had happened. She did not even know the boy, had only had, maybe, only a few words with him. Indeed, she was not even aware he was living in one of the men's apartments. She thought he lived with a friend over by the East River. His poor mother is what she was thinking. What can I say to her? What must she think of me?

Ed was preparing the morning soup, throwing in some chopped onions. There was a stack of potatoes on the table but no one was peeling. Del walked over and grabbed a potato and a peeler and began whittling away. Ed came over and put his hand on her shoulder, "Are you alright? Do you want to take off? I can do the soup and also dinner tonight."

"Tim and I saw him late last night, Ed."

Ed nodded, "Tim told me. But, he said you had no idea. No idea at all." Del thought those words true and not true at the same time.

Why did she remember him saying, "One spontaneous act"? Why remember words like that? She helped Ed for about half an hour and then decided to go up to Bellevue. Sadie came in and grabbed her arm, "Why'd my honey do such a thing? Why?" Del shook her head and shrugged Sadie off. She told Ed that she'd be back at two to prepare dinner.

Del had been sitting in the Emergency Room waiting area for an hour when Dorothy Day and Miss Bean arrived. She told them that they couldn't see Jonathan. Hospital personnel were only allowing immediate family and a priest. The press had been there but left when the family refused comment other than Jonathan's bro- ther, Ted's, terse, "You know as much as we do. Let's not make this into a soap opera." Del knew it was Ted since the physical resemblance was striking. She made eye contact as he and a woman she assumed was Jonathan's mother rushed through one door and en- tered another. But, Del was staying put. She was waiting to see the priest. She wanted to give him the letters when he came out although she didn't tell this to Miss Day.

Dorothy saw the girl glance up as they entered and thought she looked at once self-possessed and possessed. Her eyes had an unnatural bright blueness about them, something alarmed and alarming. She listened as Del told her the news. She wondered if the girl blamed her but then thought no that wasn't all of it. It was something else, some other evocation in those eyes. In any event, it was the boy's mother that Dorothy most wanted to see and not the boy. The boy was in the hands of God. Sometimes we confuse God's wishes, she thought. This was the only way she could compre- hend such a ferocious act–comprehend but not condone. Sometimes we go too far.

— 59 —

First Time, Last Time

There is a first time and a last time for every action. A first breath, a last breath. A first touch, a last touch. Sometimes you know when the last time will be and sometimes you don't. For Jonathan, it was wetness, then fire, then a roaring in his ears. Pain, profound, a red-blackness, hurtling noises, his own voice, *"Water."*

He knew the doctors were working like mad men. He heard them. He heard the words. Intubation. Shock. Vital signs. EKG. Glucose. Electrolytes. Kidneys.

What had he done?

My God, what had he done?

After hearing his own screams, someone beating at the flames. Yelling. The sirens. The terrible, terrible, abrupt and searing pain and then the red-blackness, a blankness, "Water."

Crashes and sirens and yelling. His own voice, *"Water."*

Someone saying, "Why?"

201

"I'm anti-war. All wars."

"Did you do this because of Vietnam?"

"No. This is a religious action."

What did I mean?

It was bigger, bigger than he imagined. He felt light and weightless.

He was somewhere.

Someone again, "Why this hour?"

"So no one would stop me."

What was he thinking? He went too far. But, it's done.

One, spontaneous act.

Suicide. That's what Ted will think. I can't help what he thinks. Mercedes. She'll understand but she'll be mad. So mad.

*

When the priest came out to talk to them, he said the doctors were doing everything possible for Jonathan though the situation was grave. Ninety-five percent of his body was burned but the priest said Jonathan made a devout confession and said he wanted to live. Del thought what good was that with ninety-five percent of him burned. But, she did not say this to the priest. Jonathan's mother and brother were with him and were waiting for his father to arrive. They are very upset, the priest continued, and wish their privacy. They had asked him to deliver that message to anyone who might want to talk to them or visit Jonathan. Miss Day nodded and said she understood and would keep the family in her prayers. She asked the priest to let the family know how grieved she was and that if there were anything she could do, to please let her know. The priest nodded.

The priest was young and had a stammer. Del asked if she could speak with him privately and the two of them walked out of the waiting room and into an adjoining corridor. Del pulled out the envelopes. "Please," she said. "Take these. Jonathan slipped them under my door. One is for his mother. The other, give to his brother. He might know where it should go."

Del did not want those letters. She wanted them out of her hands. The priest hesitated then took the envelopes slipping them into the inside pocket of his suit jacket. Del noticed he had the purple stole around his neck priests wore while hearing confessions or administering the sacraments. She wondered if he had anointed Jonathan's long, beautiful, burned body with holy oils.

After getting rid of the letters, she left and caught the Second Avenue bus downtown. Crumpled on the seat beside her was that afternoon's *Journal American* with what would soon become the forgotten story.

Pacifist, 22, sets self afire / outside the United Nations / flaming protest / badly burned / rushed to Bellevue Hospital / doctors said they believed he would die / police set the time of the suicide attempt by the victim's wristwatch / stopped at 5:20 a.m.

There is a first time and a last time for every action. A first kiss, a last kiss. A first time to walk into a room and a last time. A first time for a child to jump into your arms and a last time. A first time to smoke a cigarette and a last time. A first time to wind a clock and a last time that clock will ever allow itself to be wound again.

— 60 —

Afternoon

Ed looked at the clock over the sink. 2:30. He wondered if he should start cutting onions. The meatloaf should go in the oven by at least 3:30. The House seemed to have settled down for the moment. Those who knew Jonathan were in various stages of shock. Italian Mike was overheard as saying, "Jeez, the kid got me the best shirts." Ed had to chuckle. He thought that would make a good epitaph for someone who worked here. That kind of humor had saved him on more than one occasion, that and Mass and prayer, which he did regularly. The Korean War had settled that for him. He'd come back to the Church via a foxhole and, ironically, as with Jonathan, first tried a monastery and then Saint Jude's. He'd been here ten years now and considered it home.

But, he also worried about the new wave of young people arriving almost every day at the door. They were so young. Many of them never out on their own

205

before, sheltered sons and daughters. Their parents sometimes called wanting to talk to someone in charge. The phone would be passed to Ed. He would listen, assure the mother or father that the boy or girl was safe, had shelter, food, was doing God's work, the corporal works of mercy. But, Jonathan, what was that about? How could you explain that?

Ed saw Del coming through the door. She had a peculiar look in her eye. It was a look he had seen before when men were scared, not the scare of actual battle but the scare of having survived it, of finding yourself alive.

She told Ed what she knew about Jonathan. She couldn't bear to repeat the number, the ninety-five percent of his body that was burned. She said she needed to work, to keep busy and when he asked if she wanted him to stay and help, she accepted gladly. He asked if she wanted a cup of coffee before they began and she said yes. He heated up a pot, brought over two mugs, and sat across from her. As they sipped coffee, he told her about how in Korea when he got really, really scared from the noise or the silence, he'd say a prayer, any prayer, an Our Father or a Hail Mary. He didn't think about the meaning of the words. Just the words over and over. It helped.

— 61 —

Ways of Being

Jonathan

He heard every word they said and it wasn't good. There was no pain. All the nerve endings had been destroyed. But what had he done? What had he done?

His mother. His brother. The priest came and heard his confession and gave him absolution and The Last Rites. Then that priest, a man with a stammer, asked him a question no one had yet asked. He leaned over and whispered, "Do you want to live?" And, at that moment, Jonathan knew what he had not known before. He did want to live. He did not want to die. It was not dying that was important. It was burning.

*

Mercedes

The nurses knew they were not to mention anything to Mercedes about the boy who came to visit all the time having been admitted downstairs to Emergency. All of them knew it was an impossible situation. They expected him to die soon. No one could survive such trauma. It was amazing he had held on this long. Still, it was hard to go in and act normally even though Mercedes could not talk or move anything but her eyes which followed them everywhere. She could still swallow, but it was so laborious that an IV had been hooked up for nourishment. They expected the ventilator to be next. She gave them baffled and pleading looks. It was hard to be in there.

*

Ted

Ted walked down the hospital corridor to the elevators and slammed his fist into the opposite wall.

"Damn." Stupid, stupid stunt. Why hadn't he called him? Why didn't he wait? What was he thinking? Bunch of goddamn, crazy crackpots he'd gotten in with. But, Ted knew his brother. If his brother got it into his head to commit suicide, that's what he'd do. Stupid. Stupid. Hadn't he thought of that trick himself? Hadn't he gone so far as to put his service pistol into his mouth? He knew how that went. He knew his brother.

— 62 —

Dinner

The smell of meatloaf cooking was the only thing ordinary about the evening. Everyone seemed to be talking loudly or not at all. It was 4:30 and the House was filling up. Tim came over and asked if he could help. Del said, "Not now, maybe later." He shrugged, jingled change in his pocket and then went to talk to Ray and soon she saw them both go up the stairs. Ed had gone up also to see Miss Day. Del wished he would come back. There was something about how he stood and laughed and brushed his hand through his crew cut that was rooted and sane. Del heard Jonathan's name mentioned. Sadie was talking to Frances Furpiece. Mad Paul came in and immediately made a beeline for the bowl of potato and onion peelings to add to his half-filled box of bread scraps. He began his keening. "Crazy, that one. Crazy with the bums."

Ed appeared suddenly and placed his open palm in the middle of Paul's back and whispered in his ear,

"Not now, Paul." Ed was probably the only one in the House who could do that without the box being thrown.

At five o'clock all were in place for dinner. The pans of meatloaf were out and cooling. Scotty was going on about his saber wound. Italian Mike said, "Shuddup about your damn, goomba finger."

Tim put out the wooden bowls of bread and saucers of margarine. You could hear the scrape of knives on china. Ray was making sure coffee, tea and sugar were on all the tables. Ed was draining the potatoes. Del retrieved the potato-masher from the dish-drainer next to Mad Paul's elbow. She was ready for him this evening. Nothing about his wild eye could spook her more than this day already had. She handed the masher to Ed. He had already heated a pan of milk and thrown in two sticks of margarine. She checked the spinach, which was meager but drained. The meatloaves resting in their pans on the steel table were perfect. The eight rectangular mounds of beef were thick and juicy. The ketchup glaze was not dry and cracked. Ed had rolled up his sleeves and pummeled the potatoes into a perfect sheen, adding the warm milk with melted margarine, salt and pepper. Tim had the plates stacked and ready to be dished up; Ray was joking with Sadie while standing at attention, a dishtowel draped over one arm. Was it Ok to laugh and joke this evening, to wink or goof around with towels? Ed put the mashed potatoes and the pan of spinach on the steel table and Del started cutting slices of meatloaf with a spatula.

They were serving the fifth plate when the lights began to flicker. At first, Ed said, "Oh, Jeez. What now?" It was not uncommon to blow a fuse. It happened. A collective groan rose in the room, then the lights brightly surged, then dimmed again, then flickered. Del instinctively looked over to the clock. Its hands lurched, stuttered and locked at 5:20 and the lights went out.

Blackout

Standing behind the steel table, Del had the same feeling she had early that morning when Miss Bean shook her awake. Hard to explain, a calm. She walked away from behind the table, spatula in hand, gliding really, toward the front door, saying nothing to anyone. Stepping outside onto the sidewalk, it did not surprise her that the whole city was dark, totally black. No lights uptown. No lights downtown. Only car headlights glimmered, only an occasional horn. And quiet. Like the first city snowfall of the year but no snow. Only stars. New York City had stopped. A giant fuse blown. A great short circuit. Some inexplicable, transcendent attempt to communicate. That's what she thought standing there on the sidewalk. Tim was now beside her. His low whistle ending in, "Look at that."

That night the battery-operated radios reported that they were experiencing the largest power failure in history, blacking out not only New York City but also parts of nine northeastern states and two provinces of southeastern Canada. Power had gone out somewhere along the Niagara frontier. The National Guard was activated. Thousands were caught in rush hour subways. President Johnson had been notified. Sabotage was feared. The NYC Police Department summoned 5,000 off-duty patrolmen over radio station WNYC.

They ate a candle-lit dinner that night at Saint Jude's. People calmed down. They served the meal. Del cut the meatloaf with a shaking hand, her body reacting to what she was beginning to suspect.

At first, the streets were eerily quiet and absent of anyone or thing except cars, stopped or slowly moving. Drivers rolled down their windows and called out, "What's going on?" A few people started directing traffic at intersections. Car radios were turned on and the news jumped from dashboards to the street, up fire-escape landings and into apartments and back down onto the street. Candles and flashlights appeared everywhere. A game of kick-the-can got going down Forsythe Street. Free drinks were served at the Seventh Street Pub. Coffee was handed out over by Odessa's in Tompkins Square Park. Armories were opened so stranded people could sleep. Food was delivered to those caught in subways. Spontaneous parties started in apartments and spilled out onto the sidewalk. People wanted to stop and talk.

— 64 —

What He Saw

Jonathan knew he had survived longer than anyone had
expected. He heard them say that before the first crush
in his chest.

Flung out, tossed so far he could not catch his
breath. That is what it was like. In his ears, a blizzard of wings, a rushing of wind.

And, now, a great, great, quiet space.

Below. Music or chanting?

*And if I deliver my body to be burned yet do not
have charity, ...*

Do I?

Were these words taunting?

What had he done? He meant... He wanted to
say....

Someone's voice. "Ok, he's back. Hell of a time for
a power failure."

Such great space. He could never explain. Too

215

vast. Too strange. There or here, inside or outside. Somewhere.

There were the monks.

There were his parents.

There was the lake where he pulled Ted from the icy water.

The Canadian woods.

The Niagara frontier where he was born.

Why here?

Something going out of him, something coming into him.

A blizzard of wings.

Terrible, terrible crush in his chest.

It was a heart attack but the doctors brought him back. That's what they were saying. Everything was under control. It was an unusual situation but the hospital had its own emergency power. They were equipped to handle this and any other situation that could develop. They had brought him back.

Ted was listening to the doctors' voices but it was Jonathan's voice he heard.

"Don't, Ted. Don't."

What was he saying? Why, "don't"?

Ted looked at his mother. Her face was so sad.

Could anyone look more sorrowful or worn?

His father's face was in his hands.

It would be a long, long night.

But, what was Jonathan saying to him and how could he hear it?

"Don't," what?

— 65 —

After Dinner

Ray insisted Del come over to his and Suzanne's apartment after dinner to spend the night. She first resisted but then was grateful. She knew she did not want to be alone. The fact was, her thoughts were scaring her. Other people were coming over too, he said. She said she would. Ed was nodding also and so it was decided.

She saw Tim over by the door talking to a *New York Times* reporter who was doing a story on Jonathan and had been at the House for the evening meal and then had decided to stay as this newer story unfolded. Why was he hanging out here, Del thought. Snooping. Tagging along. Voyeur.

Dorothy Day was now talking to him. Dorothy felt the girl's eyes upon her. The girl blamed her. Dorothy could feel the accusation but still wasn't sure about the total charge. She thought it wasn't just that poor boy up in Bellevue Hospital. It was something older, deeper, more convoluted; maybe Del didn't know herself. Dorothy remembered when she was that age. No personal flaw escaped her fury. Leaders, especially, who made statements, espoused ideals, encouraged others to follow them had better be walking well ahead of the crowd and in full view and had best not stumble. Youth had no patience with human frailty of that order and someone like Del had scant patience even with herself.

Look at them over there, Del thought, Dorothy Day and Tim talking up a storm with that reporter. She caught Tim's eye and he motioned her over. But, no way was she going over there. No way she wanted to talk to that voyeur.

Tim thought the reporter seemed a decent fellow. He asked thoughtful questions of Miss Day about The Catholic Worker Movement, its history, its pacifism and support of draft refusal. He said he had gotten information about Jonathan from several of his co-workers but not too many really knew him. Tim mentioned that he and Del had been with Jonathan several hours before he went up to the United Nations and reiterated that he had given absolutely no indication that he was thinking about such a drastic act. Tim also mentioned that Del and Jonathan had had some private conversation prior to their all going down to Weitzman's, but he thought that was mostly about a mutual friend, an ex-nun also a volunteer at the Worker who was in Bellevue now and seriously ill. "Del could tell you about that," Tim said. "But she's pretty freaked out about all of it. She's been up since early this morning and this weird thing happened to her alarm clock that's also got her spooked." The reporter stopped scribbling in his notepad and looked at Tim. "What was it about her clock?" Tim was rubbing the stubble of his beard and squinting over in Del's direction.

"I don't know if I should say anything about it. I don't think she's too happy with any of this, you know, reporting." The newspaper man put his pen in his pocket and said, "I'm not reporting. I'm listening." Tim hesitated.

Dorothy Day was not sure why the reporter wanted this piece of information but having been one herself she knew the strange trails a story could sometimes take. Tim scratched his head and said, "Ok. Her alarm clocked stopped, the wind-up one she keeps on her window ledge. It stopped at five-twenty in the morning and when she wound it up, it wouldn't start ticking. Dead in the water. Five-twenty in the morning. The exact time when Jonathan's wristwatch stopped. They took it off him when they put him into the ambulance. The afternoon paper reported the time; that's how they knew exactly when he did it. Anyway, she thinks there's some connection, you know, in the coincidence." The reporter was quiet.

"That happened to my wife once. The exact hour and minute our first born child died. It was a brand new electric clock. It never ran again. I won't write about that but I believe in those things."

Del saw the reporter look over at her. No way was

she going to talk to that peeping tom. Gus went over
and whispered something into Miss Day's ear. They
both climbed the stairs to the second floor. Ed was
talking with Tim about foregoing Compline, saying he
didn't think enough folks were staying around to war-
rant it. Tim agreed and said he was heading over to
Ray's after he checked Scotty into the Sunshine. Gus
came back down the stairs saying he was going to stay
at the House. Although the city seemed quiet, he remembered the looting after last summer's riots and
wanted to keep an eye on the place. He asked Del
if she were all right. She thought if one more person
posed that question, she was going to list everything
that had happened in the last twelve hours and ask
what "all right" meant. Mad Paul bolted out the door
with his leaking cartons of bird scraps. After the dishes
were done and the floor swept and everyone left who
was going to, Ed double-checked the back yard shed.
Then, flashlight in hand, he and Del stepped out into
the darkened city.

— 66 —

Belief

The streets were lively though no one was shouting. Again, it seemed like a city in snowfall, only people out walking holding candles or flashlights. Strangers said hello. Every so often, a siren, but except for that, there was a hush and an orderliness. Jose was standing outside his diner and offered them cups of coffee. Ed said, "Sure." The three of them stood looking out over Delancey as an occasional car stopped and passed slowly through the intersection. Jose said he felt safer now with the traffic light out than when people were trying to beat it. They finished the coffee and crossed the Bowery. An old man hailed them from the scungilli joint on Kenmare Street and asked if they wanted to come in for a taste of grappa. He was the same old man Del saw every morning sweeping the sidewalk. She'd waved to him any number of times. They thanked him but said they were off to visit friends. When Ed took the right turn onto Elizabeth Street, Del caught his arm and said, "Wait. I've got to do something. You go on. I'll meet you later at Ray and Suzanne's."

He frowned. "Right now? I don't know. You're not going up to the hospital are you? I don't think that's a good idea, not tonight."

"No, not there," she said. "I promise. I won't be long."

Ed hesitated and then said, "I'll come looking for you if you're not at Ray and Suzanne's within the half-hour.

"I'll be there. I promise." Ed handed her the flash-light and told her to be careful.

It was nothing Del had planned. The Church of the Transfiguration was in the middle of Broome Street, a short five-minute walk from where she and Ed stood. It was the same church where Ray and Suzanne had been married. Del knew the doors were never locked. She went directly there. Inside the small church smelled of candle wax and lingering incense. A bank of ruby vigil lights flickered on the right-hand side. Hanging over the altar was the bloodied Christ. Out of old habit, Del genuflected before she slipped into the second pew from the right.

The crown of thorns bit into Christ's head. His palms and feet were nailed to the cross, his torso raked with scourge marks. This was the Christ of her child-hood and the representation that so angered her. They tried to scare or guilt you into belief is what she thought. She looked hard at that image. That night she wanted a fight. She wanted a fight with that figure on the cross.

*

Ted sat next to his brother. Jonathan had slipped into a coma following the first heart attack. His eyelids were closed but beneath them his eyes were moving. Ted could see a darting motion as if Jonathan were watching a movie only he could see. He had no eyebrows or eyelashes left but amazingly the skin of his eyelids was unscathed. It's a miracle, Ted said to himself. A goddamned miracle.

*

Jonathan thought his brother had learned very little from nearly drowning in the icy water of Tinker Lake and he also hadn't learned a thing from putting the muzzle of his service pistol into his mouth. Ted had a lot to figure out. But. Who was Jonathan Le Blanc to talk? Look at him. What had he done? He messed up. Misunderstood. Got carried away. Went too far. That's what Mercedes was thinking. Wait till I see him. That's what she was thinking. He was sure of it.

*

Mercedes was trying to get out of the bed. That's what the nurses reported. They had to restrain her. She said her legs were on fire. The words were garbled but the nurses understood. "I thought she had no feeling in her legs," one of them said. The other one answered, "It's come back."

*

Del wanted to rip Christ down from the cross. What right had He to lure them to a crucifixion? Wasn't it enough to just live? But, instead, she said a prayer through gritted teeth.

"All right. All right. You win."

"I believe in you. I believe in you. But, I will always doubt you. Do you hear me? That's all you get. That's just how it is."

Vigils

The monks had gathered for vigils. This was the darkest hour of night when the earth was most vulnerable, most in need of protection, not because of darkness but because of slumber. Someone needed to keep watch like the parent who checks on the child, like the lover at the beloved's bedside waiting for the fever to break. The monks were waiting and watching as the disciples had waited in fear but alert and together after the death of Christ. He had promised, *I will not leave you orphans. I will come to you.* Didn't the scripture say, *I will come to you?* And wasn't there a sound from heaven as of a violent wind, filling the whole house where they were sitting. And didn't there appear to them parted tongues as of fire?

The monks were chanting unaware that the Great Northeast Blackout of November 9, 1965 had been triggered only a few miles from their monastery. Some great surge of power had blown through and tripped an emergency switch in the Sir Adam Beck Generating Station on the Niagara River.

There it was again. That crushing pressure.

It was sustained and came with a rush, a beating of wings.

He was at a still point and spinning at the same time.

He saw his mother.

His father.

His brother.

His house.

He heard the dog with the jingling collar.

Bells.

The monks' chant.

He saw the little boy, Roger, his childhood friend who had gotten polio that long ago summer and couldn't walk and had to live in a great iron beast. He was here with him, wearing a yellow T-shirt, his face bright as the sun.

"I can go anywhere now," he said and sped off.

But where was he? Where was Jonathan Le Blanc?

The monks chanted. The automatic switches tripped, hurtling the darkness eastward: Buffalo, Rochester, Syracuse, Utica, Schenectady, Troy, Albany, New York City.

You will not fear the terror of the night.

They chanted.

Nor the arrow that flies by day.

A plunge of darkness across Massachusetts all the way to Boston, the dominos falling southward through

Connecticut, north into Vermont, New Hampshire, Maine, Canada, Tinker Lake, the Niagara frontier.

Where was he?

— 68 —

Fear

Del was shaking when she arrived at Ray and Suzanne's and asked only to see Ed. Tim was there also but he had the sense to find Ed. She asked him if she could stay the night at his place and if he would stay with her. Ed started to say, "Smokey's there" and then felt ridiculous and said, " Of course. Should we go now?" She nodded.

On the way to his apartment, she told him what she had done in the Church. She told him about the flutter of wings in her ear that morning, of the light appearing in the kitchen, of the clock stopping at five-twenty, of knowing somehow before Miss Bean told her that, of course, that's what he had done.

She told Ed about the conversation she and Jonathan had had weeks before in Jose's diner, how they had laughed at the idea of New York City grinding to a halt, the elevators stopping, the subways stalling, the revolving doors jammed. All stopped so that people

229

could unfix their faces and see the one another, which
is God. That's what they had said. She told Ed of
the conversation she had with Jonathan just last night.
How he had asked her if she thought someone could
take another's pain. How she had backed away from
answering. Said she didn't know. Said it was too much.
Said she had to go and his relenting, then his saying,
"Just one more thing." Just one. Did she believe there
was a God? Her irritation, her strange calm. How she
answered that she wasn't sure but she did know there
was something, some energy out there she did not understand. She felt it. But, then, she said how she could
not look at Jonathan anymore. The mist. The street-
light. How his face was way too bright. How she turned
and ran up the stairs.

She told Ed that she was afraid. She was afraid
that at 5:20 this coming morning, she would find herself
inexplicably transported to the United Nations and her
body would burst into flame. She would be consumed
as had Jonathan. The fire would be all around her
and in her and she would have no power over it. She
thought, right now, she must be crazy and she was
afraid to be alone.

Ed had his arm around her shoulders as the flash-
light caught the cement stoop of the Spring Street building. They made their way up to the fourth floor. The
building had a familiar list and smell. Ed reaching
around her put his key into the keyhole and she heard
the tumbler catch. She stepped inside as he took her

elbow and steered her to a kitchen chair. He put the flashlight on top of the refrigerator and rummaged in a drawer by the sink for a box of emergency candles that he kept there for situations. Del could hear Smokey snoring in the next room. Finding a candle, Ed lit it and placing it on a saucer said, "I'm going to warm some milk for you and then I want you to lie down on my bed in the other room and I'm going to read to you from Saint John of the Cross who understood these things. This candle will not go out until the lights come back on and you will be safe." And that is what he did.

The City

All over the city that night, the unusual was the usual. There were few arrests. Looting was not a problem. The shared experience brought out the best in everyone; there were many conversations between people who would ordinarily not have the time or take the time to do so.

Armories were opened as emergency shelters. Eight hundred thousand people caught in subways made their way to safety guided by employees with emergency lights. Thousands hiked across the Brooklyn and Queensboro Bridges. Civilians helped police guide cars and pedestrians. Impromptu parties happened in office buildings and apartments.

And, a gigantic full moon illuminated the city.

Morning

Del awoke on the morning of November 10 to the smell of coffee and toast and the muffled voices of Ed and Smokey in the kitchen. The candle that Ed had lit was still burning. Sunlight from the east window poured in warming the foot of the bed. She was in her clothes and covered with a worn flannel sheet and over that a brown army blanket. It was morning, well past five-twenty, and she was alive. She saw the chair where Ed had sat last night and, on the floor, the book she had fallen asleep to. The candle, the book, the chair, the bed, the glorious sunlight. Life itself.

Ed parted the curtain that served as the door to his room and peeked in. "Good Morning. Like some coffee?"

She felt sheepish lying there under the sheet and blanket but nodded yes. Moments later he came in holding two mugs. He looked tired and rumpled like a man who had sat up in his clothes all night, which, of course, he had.

Del sat upright with her back to the wall. He handed her one of the mugs and lowered himself into the chair by the small table with the lit candle. They sipped their coffee in silence. Del said it tasted as good as the Roma's and Ed said he owed it all to Uncle Sam. She looked at the candle and at the book at his feet. Suddenly, she felt unaccountably teary and blurted out, "I can't thank you enough for last night, Ed. Your kindness, everything. I feel foolish."

Ed bent over and picked up the book on the floor. He flipped through some pages thoughtfully and then closed the book and smiled.

"It's been a long time since I read Saint John of The Cross. It was a good night to read him. You know, people forget that he was a prisoner himself and knew about darkness, both physical and spiritual. He knew about fear and about how hard it is both for the body and the soul to move through a dark night. Certainly, that's what was happening last night."

Del felt then briefly, strongly, how grace and acceptance can visit suddenly and unexpectedly. She reached for Ed's hand. He squeezed hers in return, smiled, stood up and stretched. "The lights came on about four-thirty. It looks like a beautiful day. I have some eggs still warm in the oven if you'd like a plate."

The eggs had a wonderful flavor. Had eggs ever tasted so good? They sat in the kitchen and Ed poured another cup of coffee. Smokey had already gone over to the House. They sat in silence. Outside the kitchen window, the sidewalk's splotches of white sparkled in the morning sun.

— 71 —

Gone

When it came, it was not dramatic. A string tugging
loose, a kite hitting an updraft or wind suddenly filling
a sail, a silent scud into gone. What the body did then
seemed immaterial. The making of its noises and the
urgency and the frantic gestures were a lost language.
He was off. He rose. What more could he do, having
done what he did? He took his last breaths in this
world. They filled the sail and sent him off.

*Doctor Jacob Richards pronounced
Jonathan Le Blanc dead at 2:50 p.m.
on November 10. The cause given was
respiratory failure.*

*After an autopsy, completed about
5:30, the hospital supplemented the
earlier report, saying that the exten-
sive burns Mr. Le Blanc had suffered
had caused acute kidney failure and
shock, which had proved fatal. He was
twenty-two years old.*

And what he saw was everything.
Everything he wanted to see.
Everything he did not want to see.
His mother and father gone.
His brother finally squeezing the trigger.
His dog's empty collar.
His friends.
The children of his friends
Ray and Suzanne no longer together.
Tim married.
Gus doing hard time and harder.
Sadie happy.
Mike in a blazing immaculate white shirt.
Ed kneeling beside his bed, at 90, praying.
Del still trying to.
Miss Day silent yet speaking to him.

The monks chanting.
Mercedes surviving.
New York City continuing.

He was everywhere but he did not know where *where* was. He saw his body lying at the medical examiner's office pending autopsy. Ted was doing the paperwork. His mother and father were flying home to make funeral arrangements. His body and Ted would arrive tomorrow in Tinker Lake. But where was he? Where was Jonathan Le Blanc? He was so awake, but his body would not wake up.

Time

There is a first time and a last time to conventional time. But what happens when time resists convention?

On Wednesday the tenth of November in 1965 when Del walked home from Saint Jude's in the gusty dark, she passed the corner bodega's lighted storefront window and felt a fluttering in her ear. It's him, she thought. She looked through the storefront window to check the clock she knew hung over the cash register. It said 5:30.

"You're late," she said to herself. She walked past her apartment building and entered the darkness of the church she had knelt in the previous night. She made her fervent prayer of belligerent belief. Whatever God there was, she thought, would understand.

Acknowledgements

I first wrote about Roger La Porte in the pages of *The Catholic Worker* during the fall of 1965. Since then, in one form or another, I have been writing this book. Consequently, I have more people to thank than I could possibly mention for their attention to this story. With that said, I want to especially remember the Catholic Worker community, those living and those who have died, who were part of that world. I also want to thank the Sudden Fiction writers of Portland, Maine who first heard many of these stories in short form and encouraged me to write more. I am grateful to everyone who over the years patiently listened as I tried to make sense of what happened that night.

There are those I wish to remember who helped me in areas of research: The Mission Archives of the Maryknoll Sisters for information on Tanzania during 1964-65. Phillip Runkel, Archivist for *The Dorothy Day-Catholic Worker Collection* at Marquette University and the assistance of *The Swarthmore College Peace Collection* for its treasure trove of flyers, photographs, newspaper clippings and broadsides that documented again for me those days that were so feverishly lived.

I want to thank Rob Wood, executor of the Anna Shippen Award for women in pursuit of their creative work, for financial assistance during a crucial stage in the writing of this book.

Sections of this work were written in New York City,

in Portland, Maine, in a fishing village in Nova Scotia, in San Francisco, in Albuquerque, New Mexico and on Peaks Island, Maine. *City of Belief* in its many permutations was encouraged and commented upon by those I hold close to my heart in all of those locations.

I want to thank particularly Pat and Kathleen Jordan for their careful reading of the initial manuscript and their continued friendship, Fran Panasci, Ann Wagner, Peter d'Entremont, Wendy Wintermute, Jody Meredith and Carl Dimow for their individual reading, suggestions and encouragement that cumulatively helped me press on. Ursula McGuire I wish to thank for her invaluable telephone conversations, grit, humor and gift of camaraderie after all these years. I also wish to acknowledge the important role that Fox Print Books and Eleanor Lincoln Morse and John Moncure Wetterau have played in the publication of this book. Without Eleanor's persistent belief in the importance of this story, and John's keen editorial eye and technical skill, this book would not have seen the light of publication.